THE WORLD'S LAST WHALE

LISSE KIRK

ALSO BY LISSE KIRK

The Black Violin: A Dark Winter Romance
Wanting Less: Thoughts on Decluttering

Some creative liberties have been taken with marine biology in this book. This is not intended to disregard science, but to amplify the story.

Copyright © 2021 Lisse Kirk
All rights reserved. No part of this publication may be reproduced, distributed, or transmitted in any form or by any means, including photocopying, recording, or other electronic or mechanical methods, without the prior written permission of the publisher, except in the case of brief quotations embodied in critical reviews and certain other noncommercial uses permitted by copyright law.

www.lissekirk.com

ISBN: 9798534114072

This book is dedicated to the flappy dinosaur that encourages me so much more than I deserve. You help me believe in myself and find the courage to write stories like this.

Thank you.

1

Once I dove in sparkling water, clear and cold, salt but sweet. I danced in beams of sunlight and my songs raced before me into the unknowable depths of the sea. The water danced as well, silk against my skin, effervescent, full of life. I danced in the marriage of sunlight and seawater, what should always have been sacred, plunging down into the depths, gold and blue and green, an incandescence of life and joy, limitless illumination, light one still had faith in even when it was lost to the depths.

I danced in the water. I sang. My voice traveled farther than even my spirit could. Perhaps you would have heard clicks and whistles and trills, but my people heard more than that. They heard the life I sang, the joy, the wonder. Every day, brilliance and song. Every night, a silken darkness, a radiance of stars above us, a universe of gleaming lights below, tiny little specks of life drifting in the sea.

I sang of these things, of this beauty. I sang of storms and starlight, of moonrises red over the horizon, of sunsets flashing green as a fish's scale. I sang of births and deaths, of hunts, of love made and lost, of time.

I sang of all these things, and my people sang with me.

The entire ocean sang.

The entire ocean danced.

The entire ocean lived, thrived in this magical world—

A world we thought we were safe in.

A world we believed was eternal. Where sunlight met seawater, where starlight fell upon a marine paradise, it seemed tranquil. Untouchable.

But you.

You touched it.

Now I swim alone.

My flukes are heavy. My tail moves stiffly. My pectoral fins do not feel graceful. One cannot dance like this.

I swim alone, without dancing. I sing alone, but my songs falter and fade away.

Dancing has become mere swimming. I swim and move. I eat what little sickly food can be found and feel guilty for every mouthful filtered through my tired old baleen.

Once, the ocean was a place of abundance, plankton and krill in such density you could not imagine it, endless fish, everything one could dream of. To eat was to live and to live was a joy. Now, eating feels like stealing, taking—it feels like over-harvesting.

Exploiting.
It makes me feel like one of you.

Nights should be more beautiful when there are so few left to me, for I should cherish what is soft and rare, but they are not. The sorrow sits too heavily in my heart; even knowing that I may not make it another year, I struggle to find joy and beauty in the world around me. I remember what it once was, before you tore it apart, before you poisoned it.

My mind aches. A million memories threaten, each its own drop of pain.

I do not wish to remember.
I am tired.
I think I am ready to go.
This grieves me. I do not want to die, but I no longer want to live.

Not with what you have done to the ocean.

You went too far. I want believe we can recover from this, but I do not.

I have lost the ability to believe, to hope.
Hope.
My flukes were not made to carry anything, especially not the burden of hope. I was made to dance in it, because hope was life and life was all around me.

I tried. I tried for so long not to give up faith—
But the seas have gone silent.

Do you understand what that is like? For a creature to whom sound is more than sight, more than touch, more than simple noise, can you even comprehend what silence is like?

The ocean heard everything. Perhaps if you had heard yourselves, you would have been ashamed enough to stop in time.

Did you not know that we were listening?

Every human dream, every song, everything you were, we knew. Maybe we did not understand it, but we knew of it. How could we not? This world was one great life, one great soul, and every living thing except for you knew it.

You thought you were screaming alone, so you made the brightest lights and the loudest engines.

You thought there was nothing out there to hear you in the great void of space, in the terrifying fathoms below, so you howled and fought and railed against it all, fighting for dominion in every way you could. You had to be the loudest, the most dangerous, the most vicious. You were everything we were not, and we never understood you. You could sing, you had the capacity for such beauty, and yet you ravaged your world like a plague placed upon it before you came for ours.

I remember the seas before plastic filled them, but I am old.

Can there be any of you left who remember?

Do you remember that the sea was once a haven for all who found the courage to dive beneath her waves?

There used to be so many things to eat. No one went hungry. I remember plankton, krill, soft-bodied jellies that floated with the tides, helpless as moonlight. There were fish who darted to and fro, flashes of silver and gold, blue and green, purple.

You poisoned them.

You choked them.

How can I forgive you for this?

There was a time when your dreams were of turtles; we heard those and we hoped. You feared what would happen to the turtle, and for a time you worried about plastic, but not enough of you, and your attention waned too quickly. You took action, but it wasn't enough. Nothing changed. Not for us—and not for you. Your feverish pace of consumption continued. It grew and grew, your numbers along with it. You covered your bodies in chemicals, you filled yourselves with them, and they came to us through the water, through the runoff, until the water rushing into the sea from land no longer carried with it curious flavors and smells, but poison and toxin and death.

My people fled from yours. We sought deeper water, colder water.

You didn't let us go.

You pursued us relentlessly. Some of you slaughtered us, as you have always done, and maybe that I could forgive, for all predators are natural, but you weren't predators. You were merely ruthless. Savage. Bloodthirsty. You consumed and consumed, took and took, and what did you give us? You gave us poison water and plastic fish and reefs bleached of color and life, weak places in the sea, weak places where disease could fester.

I want to forgive you. I know I should. I don't want to die with anger in my heart, but how do I reconcile that against the aching in my soul?

2

It is night.
The moon is out.
I am far from land, but the moon still looks like it is burning. How mad a thing, for one of my kind to understand fire, but you ensured that all the world knew. You burned it all, and only when all the green was gone did you think to regret, to act, but by then it was too late.

I understand fire. I understand destruction. I understand death. Most of all, I understand what you have done to the moon. How much farther must I go to escape the way you have colored the sky? How many miles must I move my tired body, weighed down by the pain of the spirit, by the grief of the greasy, joyless water I swim through?

My eyes burn. I swim down deeper. It is colder, yes, and although it does not feel cleaner, I think perhaps there is less oil here, less poison. If I could name all the chemicals you dumped into the sea, perhaps I could have a new song to sing, a grief to sing to the stars and to the captive moon, but I do not know the names. I only know that you do not care.

I move down deeper into the darkness, but I do not sing to see my way. I do not hunt. I am not dancing. I simply swim, moving because it is all I have left to do, and I do not fear. There is nothing left here to hurt me. There is nothing left to fear. Anything that moves alongside me in the dying sea is another lost soul, another survivor, another captive, another life born into the wrong time, born to live long enough to see hope falter and fail and be washed out of the world.

Let a shark come and tear into me, let a squid come racing and sneaking up out of the darkness, tentacles lashing, hungry, great eyes gleaming. I will not fight. I will not resist. It would perhaps be better to die in such a way than to die like this, to die the slower death of hopelessness and hunger, of poison and grief.

I begin to hope for a hunter, but none come. They never do anymore. The thought saddens me. Why? Why can I not go in the natural way? Are there no predators left with the courage to act? Or has all the world gone the way of entropy and atrophy, the slow wasting away of it all?

Angry, sad, I dive.

I should have taken a deep breath. I know it as I sink. I know it, but I do not care. I can see nothing, and I descend in silence, freefall, a slow sinking. How deep can I go this time? Will this be the time I no longer feel the need to strive for the surface? Will the world's last whale sink away in silence, unremarked, unmourned, unknown?

These thoughts are self-indulgent and weak and I know it. They go against instinct, which always fights for life, but my grief is beginning to overtake that instinct. I am the last. Why should I fight to live? Who will fight alongside me? Who will know me, remember me?

I do not want to be forgotten.

There are things in the water. I feel them as I descend, moving slowly. I must be careful. There is the roughness of old fishing gear mixed with the towing and mooring lines of ships, plastic lines, rough and sharp and eternally drifting. Ghost gear, ghost gear floating in a sea of ghosts, a world of memories; grave markers.

The ghost gear threatens, but I avoid it.

I am not ready to die yet, no matter how much I wish I could accept it—or perhaps I simply do not want to die in such an undignified way, tangled in ghosts of the Earth's hunger.

The fishing gear scratches against my skin as I descend through it. I feel its tickle. There is no pleasure in the sensation. It is not like rolling in waves or rubbing against sand. There is no life in being touched by this thing.

I sink. It floats on. We part ways for now but I am never free of this invasion.

I go deeper, deeper into the darkness, the blackness. It is night above, but it is always night down here, when you go this deep. There are places in the world that light has never touched—but *you* have touched them. Humans have touched everything, their reach extended through chemicals and trash and deafening noise, and yet they feel no shame.

I'm going too far down. I shouldn't dive this deep, especially on such a shallow breath. Diving too deep without enough air to get back to the surface will end me. I know I am going too far, but bitterness stops me from caring. Did humanity care when they went too far? Or did they tell themselves they had infinite tomorrows to fix it?

I continue down, needing only small movements of my tail to descend deeper, deeper.

The water is colder here, but it's not refreshing. It's not the brisk cold of days gone by. This is the bone-chilling cold of the void, the dead cold, the cold of the grave. It presses in around me with the weight of my entire world and I feel the strain on my lungs, but something in me wants to continue down, wants to keep going, keep trying to dive, dive, dive.

It feels like I can leave the world behind.

That's the thought that finally makes me stop.

I go motionless, hanging in the water. Something brushes against my flukes. I shudder at the slimy touch, but I don't pull away. I am suspended in nothing, suspended in darkness, suspended in the depth and the pressure and the cold, so far from the air and from *life* that it shocks me.

I *can* leave the world behind.

If I go any farther, I *will* die.

My heart is beating. I can feel it. It is strong, perhaps the strongest thing here. I listen to it, to this rhythm, and I become aware of the immense silence of the depths. This terrifies me. It's so complete. Darkness and silence all around, the great pressure, the place where all things must go in the end. Even when there are tiny noises and vibrations in the water, they only amplify the silence.

I should sing. A few notes would comfort me. I hesitate, listening, falling into the trap of darkness, worrying. For the moment, my bitterness and anger towards the destroyers of the planet are forgotten as I worry. What if my voice is gone? What if I don't remember how to sing? What if the depths swallow up my sound, and my soul along with it? What am I without song?

I click. Just a few little clicks, nervous sounds, tense sounds, but they comfort me. They're something, they're noise, and they tell me that the ocean around me is not so empty. There is a human fishing boat floating, hanging motionless in a place where the seawater is dense enough to hold it until something comes along to upset its equilibrium. A wreck, a bitter memorial.

I whistle and click, short and sweet and clear, and this tells me more. I see the world light up around me in a way that can never be seen with the eyes—and I see the squid racing up from below, from the underworld. For while this water is deep to me, to them, I am still floating at the surface.

Their arms are long and grasping and their eyes are cold. For a moment I feel a stab of fear and I tense, ready to start swimming for the surface, aware that I am not a toothed whale and I will not win a fight with them, but I do not let myself move. I hang there motionless, waiting, and when three of the creatures surround me and start touching me, touching but not hurting, I begin to wonder.

Did they miss music?

Did my song call to them?

The thought makes my heart ache anew. My lungs are aching, too. I need air. I need it soon. Still, I do not move. I let the squid touch me, let their tentacles and suckers ghost over me. They seem curious yet strangely afraid.

I don't know how to speak to them. My people communicated through song, through sound, but do these things even have a language? I close my eyes and try to quiet my mind, to quiet myself completely so that I can hear it.

In the silence, I hear my heart beating louder than ever, but then I hear the squid moving, hear their soft slipping through the water. I focus on that, focus on what it is that makes them squid, on their speed, their strength, their danger, and then I begin to hear it, to hear the voices I never knew existed.

Why are you here?
Who are you?
You breathe. You come from above?
Has the world changed?
Is it better now?
Did the humans stop?
Are they dead?
Why are the seas so silent?
Where are the other whales?
Where are the ones that hunted us?
Where are the dolphins? We liked to hear them.
We liked to hear you all.
Why have the seas gone silent?

Their questions shatter my heart. What can I tell them? That the seas are silent because I am the last? My heart swells with grief as I wonder what to say, how to possibly say it, and I slump, my body going slack in defeat.

There is a gentle touch to my face. I look again, not that I expect to see anything in this darkness, but I can. The squid are flashing with a subtle light of their own, a luminescence I never knew they possessed, yet another secret of the deep. This one looks into my eye, and I see intelligence there. I see a sort of cold compassion I never expected.

Are you the last? It asks the question without saying a word.

I do not know how to communicate the way they do, so I answer in the best way that I can.

I sing.

It is one note, one long note, soft in the beginning, then mighty, growing, but then it fades out into the loneliest sound I have ever made, the loneliest sound I have ever heard, the fading voice of the last singer.

They slowly withdraw from me, their tentacles moving away. I want to beg them to stay, not to go, not to stop touching me, but my lungs ache.

The last, one says, and there is great sadness in that silent tongue.

The last.

One nudges me gently.

Go. Breathe. Sing.

I don't want to go. I protest by moving closer, by trying to put my face closer to its great soft body, but it pushes me again.

To stay in the depths is to die. You are a creature of Above. You are a creature of the air. Your lungs ache. You must go. You do not belong here yet.

Yet?

I want to ask about that *yet,* but that is just my desire to stay with them, to not be alone again.

I want to cry.

They nudge me again, and this time I obey. I angle my body up and begin swimming slowly towards the surface. There is nothing to see up there, no light to guide me, nothing to tell me that this is the right way, but I sense it. All of us who live in the ocean know our directions very well, for we feel them, we feel the water, the world, all of it around us, all the time, and we cannot lose our way.

Not unless we are already lost.

Leaving them behind feels worse than anything from recent days. It is worse than hunger, worse than swimming through poisoned water, worse than feeling the ghost gear tickling along my body, worse than swimming past land and hearing the ugly cacophony of machines and voices and uncaring abandon.

I am swimming to the world that once was peopled with thousands of voices, but is now as lonely as the depths. There are no other voices there. The life is below me, down in the deep, down in the black.

I ache to be touched again. It doesn't matter that the squid are not my kind. Their touch was beautiful. It was *real*. It was more than a memory.

The surface is a long way off yet. The ache in my lungs intensifies, spreading, making all of me hurt. The squid were right to tell me to go. My mind spins, I feel as if I am starting to see sparkles, a warning sign—

But then I realize that I *am* seeing something. It is the surface, still far above, touched with moonlight, decorated with little flashes of gold.

I remember when moonlight was white, and it was far more beautiful like that, when it was a clear and fragile light, but seeing this touches me for some reason, and I stop swimming again. I hover there, looking up at the surface, watching it dance. Sometimes the surface is very still—and that happens much more often these days, now that the water is so choked with oil that the wind ruffles do not form easily, but when the sea's surface dances, it dances with the light, too.

How long has it been since I saw moonlight dance?

Reluctantly, because this sight is beautiful and it will not be half as lovely on the surface, I continue rising. I feel my body seeming to grow lighter and stronger as the water becomes less dense around me, and then I break the surface.

I exhale a great plume, letting out all of the pressure within me, all of the used air, and then I sigh. I float there, breathing, and I watch the tiny beams of moonlight. It is too weak a light to travel far, but it is there all the same, little fingers of light stabbing down from every broken pane of sea-surface-glass, little beams of gold and orange.

These are not the colors moonlight was meant to be, but these are beautiful colors. After the depths, after too long without air, the light is still beautiful, even if it is wrong.

I lay there and look at the moonlight and I remember the touch of the squid, remember their questions. For them to be so kind, they must already have suspected the answers. Did my confirmation hurt to hear?

Although I have not felt the desire to sing in a long time, I think now that perhaps my song will make it to them. Perhaps if I sing a few notes, they will know I made it to the surface, that I made it back to the air. The thought of singing feels like too much, but for the sake of kindness and mercy, I do it.

The notes come out awkwardly, rough and discordant at first, and I panic for a moment.

Have I forgotten how to sing?

I stop, confused and hurt by my own inability, and I flounder, trying to think of something to sing about, trying to remember a song, any song, anything simple.

The moon is there above me, steady, waiting. Once my surge of fear subsides, I take it as inspiration. I try to remember the first time I saw moonlight.

I was new to the world. My mother was beside me. I was afraid of the dark that first night, but I remember her great bulk, remember the comforting presence of her, remember her love. I looked out and saw the water dancing with light, little beams of white light, and I wanted to play in it.

Don't go far, she sang to me, her voice the voice of ages, the timeless voice of love, of every mother to every child. I moved up to breathe and I floated there, moving around so easily, jostled by the waves like a little cork, fascinated by the moonlight, enamored. She was happy as she watched me, and when I nestled up against her to sleep, she sang to me, long and slow notes, long and slow and delicate, delicate and fragile as moonlight in the sea.

I remember those notes now.

I miss her.

I miss her so much.

I miss all of them.

I miss their voices. Their bodies. Their movement. Their stories. Their dances.

Why did you have to take them all away?

Why did you have to make me into this, to make me so alone?

Loneliness bites me with teeth sharper and harsher than any shark's, but I remember the notes of my mother's moonlight song and I find my voice. I sing her notes, sure I do not sound as beautiful as she did, but I sing them all the same. I imagine my voice carrying down into the depths, telling the squid of this beautiful thing they have probably never seen, telling them that I am here, I am still alive—

I am still alive.

3

I sing the moonlight song again and again. I wish I could scream, but I cannot. This is my outlet. It is the only way I can be close to my mother now, the only way to remember the others, and so I sing until my voice grows weary, watching the moon grow dim and darken as it tires, hours before dawn. The rest of this night will be dark, but all nights are so in the ocean. There is no darkness like the darkness down below.

The moon sets. The dancing bars of light fade.

Sleep begins to claim me, gentle and sweet, the only solace left in this world. Sleep steals over me and my voice goes quiet, the moonlight song fading with the light.

I try to remember my mother again. I try to feel her with me. I try to imagine she is here.

I remember you.
As long as I remember you, you are still here.
But the words feel empty; she is not here. It is only me, alone in this empty sea, and when I am silent, it feels as if I cease to exist, as if none of us have ever been.

I fall asleep, aching anew.

Yesterday's singing and my time in the depths leave me unsettled.

When I find a small bloom of krill, who are more plentiful these days than fish, yet still so scarce, I eat. There is no joy in the meal and I am not interested in eating more. I should, because this is not enough food to keep me alive for long, but it is difficult to be hungry when there is no joy in living.

I stay close to the surface, close to the light, and watch the sunlight dance, far brighter and livelier than moonlight, but also far more stark. Sunlight is a beautiful thing, turning the water to gold and green and blue. I have always enjoyed its touch on my skin. Today is no different. I enjoy the way the light dances on me, touching me through narrow bars of dappled brilliance and shadow, but I still feel unsettled.

It feels as if I am in the wrong place, or on the wrong path.

What am I missing?

I swim on slowly but steadily. I have no goal. There is nowhere I need to reach, I have no place in mind, I simply need to swim, to move. Perhaps it makes me feel more alive. Perhaps it makes me feel more foolish after the way I hung motionless below, as if I were already dead.

Am I waiting for something? It is maddening not to know, to have this sense of something immense yet awaiting me in my life, despite having already given in to grief and let go of hope. What could possibly be left to experience?

I swim through clouds of trash. Thin sheets of plastic shaped like jellyfish wiggle and float in the water. They have betrayed many a creature to their death. Plastic toys bob along next to sun-bleached plastic shards. Plastic bottles replace fish, some with caps on and so they stay on the surface, some without, drifting at different depths in the water. There are plastic figures of animals, plastic ropes. The ropes are worst of all, whether thick and rough or thin as a jellyfish tentacle. Ropes and fishing line and the sharp flat strips; these things are the apex predators of the ocean now. Ropes slow one to the point of exhaustion, fishing lines amputate, and the packing straps—those cause the ugliest wounds, the saddest wounds, before they take a life. Seals, especially, have learned that lesson.

There is plastic everywhere, a dirty, drifting cloud of it, and I swim carefully. There doesn't seem to be anything here large enough to entangle me, not today, but I do not want to die in such a way. I must die alone because of you humans; I don't want to drown because of your garbage.

Too many already have.

Its touch is unavoidable, unpleasant. Unnatural scratches, tickling, sometimes biting, sometimes sliding sensations; the ocean is so choked that none of these sensations are new.

Once upon a time, I used to be curious about the plastic. I used to look at it and sometimes nudge it to make it move, would sometimes follow along a trailing rope or net to see where it went, to see how long it was, but no longer. Now, I have seen it all. I have seen the bodies of creatures caught in those abandoned nets, seen them floating along with the trash, seen a dead shark at the end of the rope it became entangled in, drifting forever, never to be hauled in for food, never thought of by the humans who made the rope.

I have seen too much.

Now, it is all the same: poison.

The cloud of trash seems to be growing thicker as I continue on. The water has a more stagnant taste, a too-intense taste, the tang of chemicals, sickly algae, and plastic. I do not sing, not wanting to send even my meager music out into this ugliness, but I need to see what it is.

I swim until I sense that I am very close, and when I turn to look, I see what appears to be a shadow in the water some distance away.

Shadows on a sunny day are always reason to be wary, so I stop. I hover for a moment, finning carefully to hold myself in place. I look and listen, but do not yet comprehend what casts the massive shadow. I am far from land, so it should not be a boat. I am far from *everything,* out in the middle of an ocean, so whatever it is, I have the sense that it shouldn't be here.

Nothing seems to threaten me under the water, so I take a risk and spyhop to see if some threat hovers above the sea, but there is nothing in the air other than a great many gulls wheeling and whirling lazily.

There is nothing dangerous in the air, but there is something on the surface. There are even more seagulls flying over that vast rough patch, more birds than I am used to seeing, especially out here. Curious, I watch them for a moment, then sink below again and continue making my way towards the shadow. The gulls do not look concerned and so I suppose I should not be either. Seagulls are not as stupid as one might think.

The cloud of trash becomes thicker and thicker, now with tiny pieces mixed in with the larger ones, clouds and clouds of it, and slowly I realize that *this* is the shadow.

Here, in this part of the ocean, half the world's trash has compacted together to form an almost solid surface above me.

I am thirty feet down, and even here, the garbage is thick. It is everywhere, pieces small enough for me to eat if I were to attempt to filter it through my baleen, and I shudder at the thought. I know I have already eaten a great deal of plastic, tiny little pieces that drifted with my food, tinier pieces that were already in my food. I hate knowing that it is inside of me as well as all around me, but it is a violation I am helpless against.

I hang still in the shadow of the garbage, the shadow of the end, and I look around in horrified awe.

Sunbeams try to pierce down into the water, but they only illuminate the floating ugliness of humanity, the careless leftover pieces, things that can never be erased and will never be reclaimed. It is a riot of color and shapes, these things drifting at the edge of the great compacted shadow, and it could be beautiful—

If it were natural, if it were not an invasive destroyer.

Different shapes and textures and sizes of garbage in all colors, moving, drifting, a slow dance, a dance once reserved for plankton and jellyfish and other tiny lives, a dance that should have belonged to a school of fish and once did, long ago, but no more.

This dance is not for the living.

I turn enough to look up. Above me, the surface looks solid. There are fish here, taking shelter, just as there always are when something near the surface offers a protective shadow to hide in, but these fish do not look healthy. They are skinny and dull, as if they are already dead, and I understand they have little to eat here. There is some straggling seaweed trying its best, but there aren't even many living barnacles. The most prominent food there is an ugly algae, a slime that will not help them.

The covering of trash above me looks endless. It shifts and moves on the surface, surging and cracking open with the waves, with the landing or takeoff of a seagull. It could almost be beautiful, like all color and movement—if one managed to forget what it was, why it was there.

The motion reminds me of ice. Far in the north of the world, there used to be ice. I do not know if it is still there or if it has all melted away. I used to hear from the others who traveled so far and they would say no, no, the ice is gone, there is nothing left, do not go there. Others said the ice was still there but melting quickly day by day. I never knew which to believe.

The memory saddens me, and as I look at the surging, drifting darkness above me I try to convince myself that I am looking at something beautiful, that I am looking at ice.

This puts another crack in my broken heart.

It is incredible how many times a heart may shatter when the world is slowly dying. You think you have experienced the worst of it, you think you have accepted it, but you have not. Not completely. There is always one more horror to discover.

The birds seem to be mostly centered on a few misshapen, unsightly objects, and I watch them for a long moment, motionless. Things crawl on the bloated shapes from below, scavengers who must think themselves lucky, and there are fish darting in and pecking away at them in their swift, shy bites, but I imagine there is not much sustenance to be found there. It must be a bitter meal, although perhaps a satisfying one.

If I were a toothed whale, I fantasize that I would grab each of those objects in turn and shake it, bite it, beat it against the surface of the water until it falls apart, but I am not. I was born to be gentle, to be passive, which is well for those sad, rotting, discarded shapes, these human bodies; even I do not wish to desecrate the dead, however much I loathe them when they are living.

They float out here with the trash, having found their way, or perhaps they were dumped here on purpose. Either way, they belong here.

I feel bitter and ugly for thinking such a thing, but I cannot take the thought back. This is where they belong. They have made an ugly graveyard of artificial colors for us. They deserve to share it.

The viciousness of the thought makes me wince.

I am a monster.

Such bitter hatred is not in my nature. It feels wrong, so wrong—but it is easier to carry than grief. It is less heavy.

I lay still, watching the feet of seagulls idly paddle in the water as they rest nearby, fat and happy, watching their shapes. They look so alive, the only truly beautiful things here, but even they are not perfect. One has a badly swollen leg, and although I cannot see it, I know that means the bird has a piece of thin plastic line wrapped around it. Either it will lose the leg or the bird will sicken and die. The plastic found it, caught it, and so the seagull is doomed.

I hope it doesn't know, doesn't understand, but I suspect it does. I think we all know, once fate touches us, once it draws so near. One must sense such things.

I want to breathe, but I do not want to surface here, do not want to risk any of this trash coming into my blowhole.

I turn and swim out in the direction I came from, for it seems like the shortest way, and then I keep swimming, angling myself north. I put as much distance as I can between myself and the swirling shadow, the multilayered monster reaching down into the depths. My lungs burn and I am tempted time and time again to surface, especially as I am so close to it, but I wait until there are fewer pieces of trash around me. Only then do I rise up and exhale, inhale, exhale, breathe.

I rest.

I think about the discarded humans.

I am disgusted with the thoughts I had towards their bodies, but I am even more disgusted by the memory of all that plastic rubbing against my skin as I swam into it.

Plastic ghosts in seawater; that must be what dead human hands feel like.

I could confirm that, I realize, sickening myself with the thought, but I do not even consider it. I don't want to be touched like that. I don't want to look at the dead humans again. I don't want to be near them, to let myself feel such anger for them—

To risk pitying them.

I do not turn back.

I cannot turn back.

4

I rest for what feels like hours, but when my skin begins to feel hot I dive down to somewhat cooler waters. Perhaps it is the thought of ice still on my mind, but I swim north, imagining it, craving the relief of freezing water against my skin.

Does ice still exist? Or did humans burn it out of the world? Everything is warmer now than it was when I was born. Is it the same on land?

Is it worse?

For a moment I think about singing, but I instantly shy away from the thought. The only song I remember is the moonlight song from last night, and I will not sing that during the day.

THE WORLD'S LAST WHALE

I wander through the lonely blue depths in silence.

A dolphin told me once that humans crawled into large shapes and exploded towards the sky in great plumes of fire, seeking solace in the stars.

Is that what you've done? Was he telling me the truth?

Did you leave?

Did you slaughter this world, cut all the fertile life out of it, play in the remains, then grow tired of your mess and just *leave?* Are you out there among the beautiful stars, stars I can rarely see now because the sky is so often clogged with filth, congratulating yourselves on your brilliance in finding new worlds, new homes, new ways to escape what you have done?

If I were to sing now, it would be a song of anger. I feel it building within me, an ugly pressure inside my heart, but I hold it back.

I do not want to sing for you, even if it will only be condemnation.

I wander through the lonely blue.

I wander in silence.

I wander and I wonder, but I wonder with no sense of awe, with no sense of hope.

Am I still alive?

If I, who was made to sing, am silent now, then what am I? What have I become?

What did you leave behind when you rocketed into the stars? Why would you do this to me, to all of us, only to run away?

Not even a shark is so cruel.

5

All day, I swim north.
All day, I swim in silence.
I resent needing to breathe. The air feels bitter today, bitter and thin, and I do not like it. The oceans are no better to breathe, of course, for I have seen many fish gasping even in the middle depths, but I am still bitter. I don't want to see the world above. I don't want to see the smear of pollution permanently hovering over the land, all varying shades of brown and orange and toxic yellow. To live always in the depths, in the black, would be an escape, but it is one I cannot have. I am forced to breathe, forced to see what you have done. I am the witness to your crimes.

Your crimes.
Your victims.

The memory of the human bodies returns. The fingers and toes were already gone. I imagine the faces were ruined as well, or at least the eyes taken out, but the bodies still floated, so how old could they have been? When were they put there? Were they dumped on purpose? Did they simply happen into the gyre the way all other detritus does?

I swim faster than usual, and have the vague sense that something is driving me, but I cannot say what it is for I do not know. I only know that I want to swim, to move fast enough to leave these ugly memories behind. I only slow down when there are great nets or lines in the water, when there are things that would entangle and kill me and I must go slowly and carefully to avoid them, because I am not ready to be caught by your forgotten hungers.

How many other whales were? I remember the ones who simply wasted away. There were many of those, and I witnessed death after death, swimming alongside friends who did not understand why I was not failing as quickly as they were. I could give no answer; I was younger than most, but we ate the same food. We swam in the same water. Always, I had the sense of having been chosen somehow, but there was no comfort in that feeling.

I swim faster. There is no comfort in this, but it is better than being idle, better than being still.

I remember too many whales who went still.

I am the last.

I have heard every song end.

I have heard so many final breaths.

I have seen so many forms go still forever.

I have seen so many bloated bodies floating, each an island of food, a paradise for scavengers, a travesty of my kind.

I have seen too many bloated bodies, too many dead humpbacks—

And now too many humans.

Their corpses could almost have been porpoises.

I swim faster.

No.

There can be no similarities between them and us. I can't let myself imagine it. I can't. I *won't*.

I breathe only when absolutely necessary and find myself swimming faster and faster, until any other whale would think I was on a rampage—

But there are no other whales. There aren't even any rotting bodies anymore. The beluga was the last. He came south to see what there was to see before he died. He was the last I remember, and I stayed with his body for days, nudging him, clicking, begging, begging, *begging* him to breathe again.

But he became a bloated body too.

I don't want to see more. I can't. I have to escape.

I feel the memories of human bodies heavy in the water, ugly in the water, the memories of human trash plucking at my skin, and I race away from it, seeking out colder waters, waters that were always meant to be a haven. I will not reach the north in one day, nor perhaps in many, but I will reach it. I will not stay here. I will not stay so close to your great shadow in the sea.

When sunset comes, I am exhausted.

I let myself stop swimming. I float at the surface, breathing, watching the water shiver with all of those gentler colors, the beautiful colors of the peace between day and night. Below the surface, it turns black so quickly, but the surface itself is a living thing, a beautiful thing, and in these moments I can forget what you have done to my home, to your home.

The surface is smooth but rippling, always moving, always dancing. If the ocean were ever perfectly still, without even the barest hint of ripple or movement, then it would truly be dead, but it is not there yet. I have not seen a storm in a long time, but I remember the life and glory of a mighty typhoon. The thought makes me wistful, makes me yearn. I feel strange and sad and sentimental as I look at the rippling, silken panes of water. The colors are beautiful. Pale purple, rich, red as dark as blood, pink pale and brilliant, gold that dances, orange that shines. The colors do not last, they never do, but I watch them for long and wonderful moments.

Desperate for the comfort of something beautiful, I put my head above water. Perhaps the sunset will help me forget about death.

I see the clouds, swept wide and low above me, a myriad of shapes—long and soft, small and torn, tiny little ones scattered like the scales of a fish. The clouds collect sunlight on one side, shadow on the other, and it feels like I should be able to swim up into them, to swim among them, to swim in that endless seeming light—

But it is not truly endless. Nothing is.

I look at the sun.

It is low above the horizon, a rich pink, darkening to red. It fades before it ever touches the sea, and as it darkens, the world of colors goes with it.

You took the sun, too, didn't you? For these colors are beautiful, but they were brighter once, in cleaner, clearer air, and the sun did not fade.

How did you do this?

The sun sinks. There is no green flash. There is no hint of glory. I know it will come again tomorrow, but the knowledge helps little. The sunset no longer promises that a sunrise will follow.

The sun is tired, too.

I sink back into the water.

As darkness deepens, my loneliness returns, growing more powerful. I held it somewhat at bay during the day, during my race north, but my body is weary and sore and my heart cannot resist.

I long to feel other whale bodies against mine. I long for their voices, their clicks, their songs. I want to sing the moonlight lullaby, want to bring those memories back to life, but after only a few short notes, I go silent. I feel my song echoing away into the emptiness that surrounds me and it terrifies me, this blackened void, even though there should be so little left to frighten me. I do not like the sound of myself alone in such silence.

It is better to *be* the silence than to hear it.

I sink down to a comfortable depth. The moon is covered by clouds and a layer of smog is drifting over, so there is no point in waiting for it. Maybe when the moon comes back out, the lullaby won't seem so lonely.

Maybe I won't be so lonely.

How is it that the sunlight is beautiful and I love what it creates, but it is the moon that feels like a companion?

Will the moon still be there if I reach the north?

Thinking of the moon, I fall asleep without realizing what I am doing. I surface and breathe, but I am sleeping. My mind goes quiet, my heart slows down. Perhaps there will be peace in sleep.

6

The darkness begins to glow all around me. The glow is eerie, strange. It is not a true light. It shouldn't exist in the ocean, not on its own, but it is captivating and beautiful.

All around me, points of golden light form, slowly growing brighter, spreading, gleaming, wonderful. I watch them, feeling utterly hypnotized. I can see every little movement of the water, every swirl, every pulse. They are brighter than plankton, but I do not know what else they could be.

What light is so bright?

I yearn to know and cannot help feeling that they beckon to me. I focus on a patch of lights and they start to come together, to take a form that feels painfully familiar, although it is still too vague for me to understand.

I swim closer. The lights grow brighter and brighter, the form becoming more solid, and by the time I am surrounded with light I want to cry out in joy, for now I recognize what they have become. Now I see what they are.

Whales.

All around me are the heavenly forms of whales, dolphins, and porpoises. Their bodies give off golden light and although I cannot touch them, I do not feel alone. They are looking back at me and the exquisite joy of simply being *seen* floods through me.

They know me and they see me, and as I swim between them, lost in this trance, lost in the wonder, they begin to sing.

Each has a song of its own, a story of its own, a voice of its own, and perhaps so many voices should be discordant, but they are not. This is a beautiful harmony. Their songs make the water vibrate. They caress me, cleansing away the memory of plastic's touch and the shadows cast by unwanted corpses, cleansing away the loneliness of these long years. They vibrate through me, touching my heart, my mind, my lungs, my veins, every part of me.

Their songs are eternal, beautiful. Their voices are otherworldly. These glowing whales, these spirits, they are so dense in the water that I can barely swim between them, so I go still. If only I could weep, you would perhaps understand my grief and my joy, but I cannot.

I am surrounded by light and sound and stories, songs eternal, notes I had forgotten existed, music that dances, music that lives even when the singers do not. They love me. I feel it. They love me, they see me, and they are waiting for me.

When my time ends, when my life ends, I will go to them. I will be with them.

I will sing with them.

Waking from the dream feels harsh, and I let out a single keening note of pain, of grief, when I realize that's all it was. My body bends, drooping, and I cry out again and again, shrieking my loudest notes into the sea as if that can help, as if they can still hear me—

But they can, I realize, and my spiral into despair suddenly halts.

That was the message of the dream.

They are there.

I cannot see them. I cannot *hear* them. But they are there. They see me. They hear me. I am alone, but I am not alone. They are waiting for me—

But they did not beckon me to join them. I remember that suddenly. They know my pain, they know my grief, my heartache, but they did not ask me to come to them, they did not welcome me.

Not yet.

Not yet.

There must be something left for me to do.

I hang in the darkness, shocked, considering this, then slowly rise to the surface. I breathe deeply, then look at the stars. The moon is slowly coming out from clouds, shining through, so the stars will soon fade out, but the air is shockingly clear now and the stars are brilliant, an endless sea of light above me, mirroring the sea below. Pollution usually makes the night sky too thick to see through; this light feels like yet another gift.

There are as many stars as there were spirits.

The thought makes me yearn for something, makes me want to cry out, and I look for as long as I can before feeling the need to sink into the ocean again.

For the first time in a long time, it feels as if the ocean is cradling me, as if it is holding me with love, not simply carrying me along.

Into the darkness, the memory of all of those songs still alive within me, I begin to sing.

It is a sad song, a mourning song, a song all my people have always known, a song I once sang often when we began to die, but now it is only my song, and I will sing it all the night through. It is my song, and it is more beautiful than it has ever been.

A mourning song, after all, is a song of love.

7

Human lives are like waves, insignificant but ultimately destructive. Brief. Sometimes intense, sometimes unremarkable, but always relentless. They cannot be stopped. They are everywhere. They affect everything. But ultimately, each is blessedly brief.

My life is not.

It feels like I have always been alive. I feel ancient, yet at the same time I feel very young. Is this what it is to grow old? The body ages around you, the world grows dim, and yet inside you feel younger than ever, new and childlike and frightened, alone in a world that has moved on without you, in a world where all you loved is already gone?

A new fire burns in me, ignited by the dream, smoldering in my unquiet heart. There *is* something more out there for me to find, and I will do whatever I must to get to it. I will try. I will try until it kills me.

I continue swimming north every day. Every night, once the moon is out, I wake and sing the moonlight lullaby and then the song of mourning. The two are starting to become intertwined, merging into one new song, one even sadder song. When I sing one, it becomes the other, and although I remember what each song should be on its own, I do not try to stop them from becoming one.

Mourning and moonlight are each made sweeter by the other.

I swim every day. I do not stop to eat. There is not much here anyway, so little left, and when I do find food, often it does not feel worth it. It seems wrong, somehow, to eat when I am the last, when I can feel my people so close, their spirits waiting, the memory of that dream a gleaming beacon of hope in my heart.

I know this is foolish. If I do not eat, I will die, and then there will be no one to remember the whales, the porpoises, the dolphins. There will be no one to remember the songs, no one to remember the gentle grief we felt when humans chased us down and punctured us with brutal harpoons, no one to remember our helpless horror as pollution spread, unstopping and unstoppable. All we could do was watch. Watch and die. We couldn't fight.

We were always gentle.

You never were.

I should not forget this. I must not. I cannot.

8

I swim north.

For a long time, nothing changes. The water is the same, listless and nearly lifeless. There are more patches of garbage, more fishing gear to avoid, more derelict vessels. Your reach has extended everywhere, it seems, and I shudder at some of the horrors I pass.

How could you do this? Everything you have ever done to my people, to my home, how?

Maybe you could believe that fish didn't have feelings, they were so alien to you, but whales? I breathe air, just the same as you. I drank milk as a baby, I was comforted by my mother's voice.

How were we ever so different that you could so easily engage in genocide? Why did you never stop to think? Why were those few voices who protested never heeded?

Did you even flinch?

Shouldn't songs of mercy and compassion be the most precious, the most important? Why should any being possess intelligence if not to use it in kindness?

I am too angry to sing during the day, when I can so easily see everything, see your ghosts and your poison, but as I continue swimming north and nothing seems to change, that anger starts to soften, or else I am wearing down.

Should I forgive you, I wonder? No. No, I do not think so. I do not think you deserve forgiveness, but perhaps I can let myself feel compassion. Perhaps I can hope that you will not go extinct as we have done—

Well, as we will do soon enough.

No. Compassion is too great a gift. I must resist offering it. I must.

Nothing changes. I swim and I swim, always going north, and nothing changes for the longest time. A new song is taking slow shape within me, but I do not give it voice yet. I let it grow, nurturing it, for this song is a creation, not a memory. This is *my* song, the song I wish you had heeded, the song I wish you had sung, for this is a song of mercy, this is a song of pleading.

This is the song I wish could have saved my people.

When it is ready, I begin to sing. The notes are low and sad and heavy at first, but then they slowly grow higher and sweeter, cleaner, purer. My heart is in them. My heart bleeds. I sing out this plea, although it is far too late, and it echoes down through the depths of the ocean, racing out ahead of me, following close behind.

My confidence grows as I hear this beauty spreading throughout the sea, and I continue singing, singing my plea for life even as I move through the trash, even as old fishing nets scrape against my skin. I sing into the silence, filling it, and I wish you could hear me. I wish you could understand. This is the most beautiful thing I have ever sung, perhaps the most beautiful thing any of us ever have, because there is nothing but desperate, unrestrained feeling in this song of pleading, in this song of grief, of begging, a song made of moonlit lullabies and lost souls and remembered friends and uncounted, uncountable, unavoidable, unnecessary deaths.

 I am singing to you.
 You do not hear me, I know this.
 Still, I am singing to you.

 Perhaps I have gone far enough, or perhaps there is some magic in the song, for one day, things around me begin to change. I detect a current of cooler water, water that somehow seems cleaner, and it brightens my heart. I have not eaten in a long time now, but find the energy to quicken my pace anyway, excited by this hint of relief.

 I am still singing; the song is constant now, with me everywhere I go, this song of mercy. In these notes are the stories of every whale I ever knew, every memory, everything I have felt and known and experienced. I sing alone, with no one to truly understand, no one to hear. As my love for singing returns, so too does my long-forgotten conviction that music is still music even without an audience.

 How could I have stayed silent for so long? My silence means nothing to you, it is a mark of your ugly victory. But my song? I pray that one of you will hear it and feel shame, a deep shame, a shame that twists like a knife, a shame that aches in such a way that you cannot ignore it, cannot pretend it isn't there. Feel shame, shame enough to take action, shame enough to try and stop the spread of all your human cancers and poisons so that those who come after me have a chance to live. It is too late for me, too late for the whales, but there are still seagulls, there are still seals. There are still fish and squid and jellyfish. Fewer and fewer of them every day, and they do not breed well, for all the oceans are dying, but can you not find a way to give them mercy? Can you not give them kindness in the final years of their life? Can you not learn to appreciate the beauty of the ocean now, all of you, not just a few rare dreamers, so that while there is still *life* in it, you can love it?

Despite these thoughts, there is no hope in my song. You have not taught me to hope, only to fear and mourn and accept. My song is an accusation, a declaration of love, a memory, a revival, a calling to ghosts, a ballad of regret, and it is poignant and beautiful, but it is not hopeful.

Not until I encounter the colder water.

When I find a current that chills me, I stop swimming. I stop singing. My voice echoes away, floats away, and I am stunned, for I had lost hope that there might be truly cold places left, that there might be water that almost tastes clean, water where I don't see oil's deceptive rainbow sheen everywhere.

This current is narrow but strong, clean and cold, and as I lay in it I shiver, stunned. I am too thin, this cold water is a shock, but I love it. I let out a single note, a new note, a note with only one meaning:

Hope.

It stuns me.

Hope.

Is that what it feels like?

I surface and spend a long time breathing, moving my tail only enough to keep myself stationary in the current, not wanting to be carried away, and my mind reels.

Hope?

How can such a thing touch my heart again?

Why does it hurt?

When I have rested, I continue swimming. It is more difficult to swim into the current, but the cold water feels cleansing. It feels like its own reward. It feels exhilarating, and I find myself swimming faster, swimming gracefully, and I feel beautiful again. I feel like a whale, like a stunning creature, like the graceful dancer of the depths I was born to be. I am too weak to leap, but I want to. I very much want to.

Instead, I repeat this one note, this note of hope.

It is the sweetest note I know.

Moonlight and mourning are memory. Hope does not replace bitterness. It does not replace grief. It does not erase the unspeakable heartache and pain. Hope does not make anything better. It is soft and subtle, dangerous perhaps, something I did not understand until now.

Hope is more precious than a pearl.

Hope is daunting.

Hope is buoyant.

Hope is cold water.

Hope is minutes that pass without seeing plastic.

Hope is terrifying.

Hope is the potential to be hurt again.

Please, do not hurt me again.

The cold current does not last long enough. When I lose it, when the water is tepid and lifeless once more, I feel a grief deeper than all the rest settle into me. I stop swimming. I hang limply in the water, hurting, tired, sad, and I do not sing.

Did you not know you were going too far?

Were there no signs that you should stop?

Were there no wise ones screaming at you that the world was a beautiful and fragile place and you were carelessly destroying it?

Didn't you know what you were doing?

You had language. I know you had language. I have heard you speaking to each other before.

How could you not have known?

How could you not have cared?

I do not know where my hope has gone and I feel a flash of shame at being so weak, at not being able to hold onto such a fragile, beautiful thing.

Days of swimming pass in a blur, my thoughts flowing from anger to hope and then to pain, but then the ocean around me begins to truly change and I am pulled out of myself.

The water is cooler, cleaner, and not just in small currents. It is not clean water, not untouched, not cold, but it is cooler and cleaner and that is enough to ease my mind and heart. I swim quietly and more calmly, and when I find food, I eat. Every so often, I stop and listen, hoping that up here, where things are better, there will be something, some note, some song, some hint of another like me, but there is nothing.

I should know better than to hope, know better than to listen, but this cooler water makes me feel like myself again, as much as I can.

Tonight, I will sing. I will sing the moonlight song and the mourning song and if I can find the strength in my heart, I will sing the note of hope.

9

I am closer to land now. I swim towards it. It looks harsh, a rocky shoreline with something dark above it, and as I get closer I realize that the darkness is *trees.* It shocks me, for it has been so long since I have seen any that were green, any that looked alive and well and weren't artificial. Perhaps I have been too long in southern waters, but seeing these feels so sweet and unexpected that it hurts.

Even more shocking, there is abundant life here in the water. Not everywhere, but when I swim into a bay, moving carefully through the sharp piles of rocks at its entrance, it is all around me. This pocket of the ocean seems untouched. There are starfish on the rocks. There are colorful sea anemones waving their little tentacles cheerfully in the dappled sunlight. Hermit crabs roam freely, fish dart to and fro, and Dungeness crabs walk along the sandy bottom. There are barnacles, too, and not just the tiny, sickly, weak-shelled ones I have gotten used to seeing, but giant barnacles, ones the size of a human's fist. Their feathery feet are beautiful and soft looking when they sweep out to feed, and I watch them in awe. Sculpins dart near the bottom, seaweed and kelp grow everywhere, and I do not know where to look.

Is this real?

It cannot be.

It cannot be!

This is what the ocean once was!

I turn carefully, aware that this bay is really too small for me; I can swim from one side to the other in just a few powerful strokes if I choose to. I look around, taking it all in, feeling a sense of absolute wonder. This bay is alive. Looking out beyond it, between gaps in the rocks, I can see that the ocean is just as dead out there, and I do not understand how this can be.

Waves rock me. I love the sound of them hissing up the coarse sand beach. I float in the middle, taking it all in, and as I do, I start to notice differences. They are subtle at first, but once I learn to see them, they're all I can see.

The seaweed is different here. The shade of green is different, more vibrant, almost the color of some human plastic, such a bright green it almost hurts to look at. The Dungeness crabs appear to be what one would expect, but their eyes have gotten much larger, their legs longer, more spindly, and their claws are thicker than ever. The fish are different too— perhaps in them, the difference is the most noticeable. Their colors are wrong. Fish that should be brown instead look purple, others look gray. Unlike the seaweed, their colors are not as bright as they were, and their bodies look longer, more slender, more streamlined. These fish are not fat and well-fed, not compared to what they should be, but they are healthy enough for their new bodies.

The starfish are different, too. They look smoother, more rubbery, and they too have developed longer, thinner arms.

What does this mean?

Is life changing so quickly in this bay? Is it natural? Was it some poison dumped into the water here? The only thing that looks the same are the giant barnacles, those ancient, impressive creatures, and I cannot help but wonder, will they survive? Will they breed true? Or will their offspring change, as everything else in this place has changed?

What am I seeing? Is this survival, or is this defeat? Why here?

I float and rest, overwhelmed, trying to take it all in, and I let the waves comfort and rock me, let their soft susurration lull me into half-sleep. As I wait, fish dart out to explore me, nervous at first, just as they always have been, and then they become bolder. They peck at my skin, finding little things to eat there, lice and barnacles, and I hold very still, enjoying this, somewhat shocked by it. Like the touch of tentacles in the deep, this contact feels alien, but it is welcome. It is so very welcome.

Tentatively, I let out a few quiet little clicks, not wanting to be silent, not here, not in this beautiful place. Everything in the bay freezes at once, shocked by this alien sound, and I feel frozen too, a little ashamed. Did I frighten them? I meant only to greet them. Ashamed, worried, I wait in silence until all of the little creatures begin moving again, and then I let out a few more clicks.

This time, although I can sense them looking at me and wondering, no one is frightened. My heart thrills.

Yes! This is how it is meant to be! No one should be frightened of my song. My voice was made to be beautiful, not to be an instrument of fear.

Excitement surges through me and I let out a few careful notes, quiet notes, little notes, and with each one, I capture more and more attention. They are listening to me, watching me, and I think they like me. Emboldened, I make myself remember the note of hope, that sweetest of all notes, and I sing it out, pure and sweet and bold, and let it echo around the tiny little bay of life.

Creatures begin moving towards me. Hermit crabs look up from down below, distracted from their endless fighting and foraging. Fish swim close. A jelly drifts by, oblivious as always, and I feel a rush of love for that beautiful thing gleaming in the sunlight.

They have all gone still again, save for that jellyfish, and I wonder if they are afraid, but I realize they are not. Frightened fish do not edge closer. Frightened crabs do not simply stand there, claws at their sides.

I sing the note again, then again, and I think perhaps my heart will break, for it is far more beautiful to sing when other living things can hear.

Soon, I begin to sing the moonlight lullaby, to mix it with mourning, but now I also mix hope in with that sweetness and grief, and the raw beauty of the song makes my soul ache.

Everyone listens. Birds have landed in the water. Some are standing on my back. All are still. All are listening.

Oh, you beautiful creatures. Has it been so long since you have heard a voice like mine? Has it been so long since you have seen a whale?

Am I as new to you as you are to me? Do your eyes behold a monster, a behemoth, a god? Or can you see how frightened I am, how alone, how sad?

The World's Last Whale

Do you think I am beautiful? I hope you do, for to me, you are the most beautiful of all. I would like to be beautiful with you.

When my voice fades off, the creatures return to what they were doing, but something about them somehow seems calmer, more orderly. I feel content, pleased with myself, pleased with the song, and I feel for a moment that I belong here, that this is a *good* place. I know I cannot stay for long, for the bay is far too small and the food here would never sustain me, but I decide to stay through the night. The sunlight here is beautiful; perhaps the moonlight will be as well.

I hang at the surface, content, and let my mind wander. I doze off, but not for long; suddenly, there is something touching me. I twitch, surprised but not frightened, and look to see a seal in the water with me.

It is a beautiful thing, silver with black spots. It is too thin, as am I, and it does not look like the new life of this bay, does not look as if it is adapting, as if it is changing, and so I know that it is from my world. It is from the past, from the age that must die, and this saddens me, but I am glad to see it.

It swims alongside me, rubbing its soft little body against me as it goes, exploring, snuffling, tickling. Sometimes it brushes me with its feet and I feel the little hidden claws, but I don't mind. I wait patiently, letting it explore me, and when it seems to have finished and it swims up near my face, I click at it in as friendly a way as I can manage.

The harbor seal responds by simply climbing up onto my back.

I am elated. It has a beach, it has rocks, it has so many places it could climb out of the water, but it chooses me! The seagulls must be offended for there is some shifting and irritated squawking, but they make room. I feel that tiny little body wiggle around until it finds a place it seems content, next to my blowhole, and then it settles down.

I let my mind drift again. This is bliss. This is the purest joy I have felt since the dream. Until you have been isolated, you cannot understand the true depths of loneliness and pain. The mere presence of another creature can be validating, reassuring—a comfort.

Thinking of the dream hurts, casting a shadow in my heart, but this is not a moment for sorrow. In this moment, I have a beautiful little friend and I feel something close to happiness.

10

The seal leaves at sunset. I miss it, but do nothing to try and stop it. I can hear it moving around, turning things over on the seafloor. It is hunting. It gladdens my heart to know that the seal, at least, is still trying to eat, trying to live.

When the moon rises, I sink down deeper into the water, disturbing the birds who had been sitting on me. I do not go all the way to the bottom, but I float near it, surrounded by ocean, surrounded by life, and I fantasize that this is not just one tiny pocket. For a moment, I let myself believe that this is the entire ocean, that there is life everywhere, hope everywhere, that all of the beautiful things in the world are still thriving, that they're not dying off.

Moonbeams shiver and dance their way into the depths. Creatures look like ghosts as they walk across the rippled sand below.

I sing.

I start off slow, as subtle as I can, holding myself back. The notes are sweet and tender as I begin the moonlight song, but when I weave in the first note of hope instead of a note of mourning, my voice strengthens. I sing and I sing, crying alone in this beautiful place, this place that by its very existence promises the rest of my ocean must falter and die, that the balance has been tipped, that the old will not survive. I sing beautiful things, my heart filling with the grief, with the hope, and I craft every song as sweetly as I can, sending music wrapping around rocks, dancing with the beams of moonlight, shivering in between the fronds of kelp.

Everything seems to go still and listen. Everything is in awe. I feel all of that focused energy, feel all of those minds, those little sparks of consciousness and life and beauty, all listening to me, considering me as they did earlier, as if they had forgotten I was here. I sing new songs, songs made of hope, hope and grief and sorrow and joy, because that is what the life in this bay deserves. They are survivors. They have a chance. I do not. I do not, and so they must carry this magic, the magic of song, into the new world. I must give them this music to weave into their memories.

Clouds cover the moon. The tide changes. The water coming in is warmer. It mixes with the cold and I go quiet, for something is stirring.

Light.

Bioluminescence. Phosphorescence.

Beauty.

I watch in awe as light gleams, the softest blue, a blue so delicate it almost feels as if I am not truly seeing it. The surface of the water shines. Every wave shimmers. Light glitters and dances in the depths, and sparks go off as the tiny plankton touch the rocks, the seaweed, even the seal as it darts to and fro.

I am silent, but I do not feel silenced.
I feel as if I have been answered.
This is the song of the sea.
Whether or not it heard me, this is its answer.
Light. Life. Beauty.
Hope.

I sing the note of hope once in reply, clean and pure, and all the water around me shines brighter for a moment, until the sound fades.

I watch until I must surface and breathe, and as I move up through the gleaming water, the water possessed by this tenderest of magic, I feel like a creature made new.

The bay is too small. I cannot stay here. It is too small, and it is not for me. The Bay of Life is new and delicate and if I stay here even for a few days, I will change it in ways that perhaps it was not meant to be changed.

I am not like the humans. I care about this.

So, although I wish I could stay, although it is beautiful to be surrounded by such an abundance of life, even if it would once have been the bare minimum for living creatures in the sea, I move on. I start swimming before daybreak, uncertain whether I will be able to make myself leave if I wait for dawn.

The sky above is gray and silver and streaked with clouds. The water is dark gray, almost black.

The sea takes longer to acknowledge the brightness of day than it does the darkness of night.

I swim away without looking back, although my heart begs me to, begs me to reconsider, to turn, to listen, to go and look at all of that life one more time—

But my decision is made.

I still feel the calling to continue on to the north, to find colder waters, to see if there is still ice, to just go and go and go, to see what else there is. Perhaps there is a time when I will turn around, perhaps nature will decide for me when I am done, when my strength gives out, but until my journey north ends, I must continue to swim.

The dawn is quiet and gray. I am grateful for that. It feels appropriate—a grey dawn to reflect the grayness of a heart leaving behind the most beautiful place she has seen in a long, long time.

I need quietness to comfort myself, to combat the grief that comes from understanding such a tragic beauty.

11

As I swim through the day, I begin encountering small blooms of krill. I want them, and I move towards them once, intending to eat, but something stops me. There is something slightly different about them, and I am not sure what it is. The color? Their size? Their density? The way they move? Something is different enough that although I cannot place it, it stops me. These krill belong to the new world, the world of the Bay of Life.

I do not.

So, although my belly is empty, although instinct says *eat,* I move on; I am more than just a creature of instinct now. I will not take what is not mine.

I will not become like You.

When I have gone far enough from the Bay of Life that I do not feel tempted to turn around—or at least far enough that the temptation is not so difficult to resist—I start singing again. I sing the same few songs, slowly, softly, as I swim alone through waters that have once again gone empty and quiet. I move as slowly as I swim, always listening, always hoping—

Always hoping.

I am trapped in hope now, now that I have felt it. I am trapped and it will be with me until the end.

12

After several days and nights of this slow trek, I find myself in a tidal current. I relax into it and let it carry me, for I tire more easily now than I should.

The current feels gentle, and even better, it is cold. I let my mind and voice go quiet. I float. I listen to the water. I listen to the little things, the movements of distant rocks shifting, the waves. I am still close to land, and I can hear the wind in the trees, for there are trees here too, a dark blur of wilderness that has somehow survived. It amazes me to think that humans have not covered this place completely, that they have not ripped out every last tree in order to put up apartments and flashing signs and roads that radiate heat. Even at night, there are no lights here.

Why?

What is different here? Surely they did not leave this place untouched because it is beautiful. What is it about this place that changes the animals who call it home? What is it about this place that makes it feel so empty, but that still allows it such life?

Did you do something to it?

Did you put some mysterious poison here, something that cannot be seen or felt or tasted? What have you done?

Whatever it is, I am glad. I am glad you left this place to be wild, even if most of it is fading. I am glad to have hope, whatever it may ultimately cost me.

The current carries me closer to land. I hang listlessly in the water until waves begin to rock me. I hear them crashing against rocks, but there is something unusual in the sound. Letting out a few clicks, I discover that there seems to be another bay some distance ahead of me, a long and deep one, a finger of ocean cutting into the land.

Intrigued, I start swimming towards it. Perhaps this, too, will be a bay of life—

A new and alien world.

The entrance to the bay is narrow. The water is deep. Even the bright sun of the day cannot cast its illumination far here; the water is a rich living green for only a few feet, plunging quickly into blackness. Above the fjord, the walls of earth are high and harsh, sheer rock cliffs so tall and steep that there are no trees on them.

It feels quiet here. The waves are powerful, rolling against the land in deep swells, rocking me, but most of their power shoots past the entrance, leaving the waters within very still, save for a swift eddy at the mouth.

Something about this place frightens me, but I do not know what it is. I see nothing to fear, no hazards, no threats, no predators. Even if there was one, I might welcome it.

So why am I frightened?

What is it about this fjord?

My heart cautions me against it. Instinct cautions me. There is something here that I am perhaps not ready to encounter, but I do not heed the warning.

I am not on this journey to be safe.

13

I enjoy the feeling of the eddy as it swirls around me, but I am through it all too soon and I continue on into this inexplicably foreboding place.

At first there is nothing. I sink well below the surface, down into darker waters, all the darker here for the narrowness of this place, shadowed by high walls of stone. I move slowly, cautiously, looking and listening, swimming in my old silence.

When I make it to a kelp forest, my heart stutters and my mind seems to go blank. For a moment, I cannot believe that this is real. I must be imagining things, because this cannot be. The last of these places was wiped out years ago.

It is *beautiful.*

All around me, dense and vibrant and fiercely alive, there is a mighty bull kelp forest. These were our great forests once, long ago, before they were all ripped out or poisoned. These were safe-havens, refuges, places of wonder and ease and constant change.

This kelp forest feels young, new, but voracious. After a few moments of looking at it, I see that it is different from the forests of my memory. The kelp itself has changed. The fronds are longer, narrower, the green brighter and almost toxic looking, but I don't care. I am in awe of its presence.

It reaches all the way to the surface and when I look, I see the floats bobbing there. I see birds swimming, their little feet paddling innocently along. There are sea lions, their bodies dark and thin and swift, their coats ragged. I can see their bones through their fur, see their hunger, and I see that the fish they are chasing are like those in the Bay of Life—changed. They are too swift, the sea lions cannot catch them.

This place feels strange. Unknowable. It is not for me. I cannot explain it, but I know that I am an interloper. I do not belong in this fjord, which is in the middle of its transformation. I know, yet I remain. I hang there, fascinated. I drift into the kelp forest to feel it brushing against me, caressing me, that soft slip-slide of the strong plants. Being here feels like a dream. I move carefully, but I do not go in very far. Even in my thin state, as hunger takes its toll on me, I know that I am too big; I may damage this beautiful, strange, new, toxic place.

Life is finding its foothold here, grabbing onto the rocks with the tenacity of this new and ferocious kelp, these strange new fish that cannot be caught by the old predators.

The water is dark throughout most of the fjord, but in the center, sunlight trickles in. It shines down through the kelp, illuminating its hypnotic sway and dance, and it pains me that I cannot weep at such beauty.

When the world is ending, no matter how slowly, it is painful not to be able to weep at all.

As I watch the dance of the kelp, as I take in the beauty of this strange new world, I feel my death beginning. It will be slow, but it is here, settling into me. Death. My death. I am so much closer to the end of my story than I ever realized. The thought saddens me, but I try to take joy in knowing that not everything is ending; new lives are taking shape in these unexpected places. It is strange and almost frightening. It is beautifully defiant. It is strong. It lives. It will change. It will adapt.

I will not.

I will end.

When I sing here, curious to see what it will sound like in the forest, everything scatters. Fish and sea lions, they flee. I do not understand why, why they fled from just a few mournful notes, but I do not attempt to sing again.

I turn to go.

Moving carefully, slowly, sadly, I swim out of the kelp forest. I swim along the sheer rock wall, as close to it as I can get, and I look at the creatures there. They are not as abundant as in the Bay of Life, but they are lovely in their own way. Most of them, I think, will be here long after I have died. These barnacles, these starfish, that scuttling hermit crabs, all will remain. Those snails, the sponges, the soft coral, the grotto of anemones tucked away in a crevice, barely illuminated by a beam of sunlight, but gleaming in all their brilliant color, will outlive me.

I will be gone soon, and they will be here.

Is it wrong to grieve one's own death?

I leave the fjord.

The current has abated. The tide stands slack. I move back out into the open ocean and I put some distance between myself and the fjord before I begin to sing again.

These first few notes are heavy. They are the notes of grief. The notes of my own death. No one else will sing a song for my death, so it is up to me.

I sing my song and it dances away into the haunted depths, echoing behind me into the fjord. I was a brief and frightening moment for this strange place; I do not wish to be anything more sinister than a memory.

Whatever the fjord will become, let it grow in peace.

14

When I can no longer hear the sounds of the fjord, I feel as if I have escaped something, as if I am free again. My heart lightens and I sing, and once I start singing, I do not wish to stop.

Everywhere I go, I sing. I sing my own death song, and I sing mourning for everyone else I have known. I sing everything. Every lullaby, every memorial, every story, every song. Everything I can remember, I sing.

The strange chill of the fjord stays with me, the hope and beauty of the Bay of Life remains, and I sing. With these notes, I give all that I am and all that I have ever been to the sea. I give all of my people to the sea. I consign us to the depths, to the darkness, to the dance of light and water; perhaps the sea is not as beautiful as it once was, but it is all I have. It is enough. There is hope here, and hope is enough.

I swim and sing and swim and sing. Sometimes I stop and listen to rocks falling into the water or to the crash of waves, to the rolling of pebbles, to the cries of the gulls, but I can feel my time running out as quickly and surely as the tide ebbing from a shallow bay.

As long as I swim, I sing.

As long as I sing, I live.

Even with no one to hear me, I still have a voice.

Even with a failing body, I still have a heart.

Even without hope of a future, I am still me.

I swim. I sing. I dance in the depths, alone. I roll in the waves, alone. I watch seabirds and clouds, alone.

I am caught between the strangest, sweetest mix of joy and despair, which together are perhaps the beginning of acceptance.

I am alone.

I am free.

In this moment, I am not unhappy.

Slowly, I begin to realize that my anger is fading. Humans are no longer a presence that seem to always be with me. Before, I raged against them, furious, betrayed, and heartbroken. Here, where there is hope, where I have found this strange freedom even in the slow wasting of my body, the anger fades. I still grieve, but I no longer feel as if I must direct my hatred towards them. I no longer feel as if they are with me, hearing me. I no longer need them to.

The seals that do not change will die.

The fish that do not change will die.

The seaweed that does not change will die.

The starfish that do not change will die—

And the humans that do not change will die.

They must know it. Some of them, at least. Perhaps most of them are still too wrapped up in their lives of meaningless light and noise, believing that the distractions given to them by technology are a substitute for living, but there must be some who sense this sea change. There must be some who know that if they do not adapt, they will die.

I do not yet have empathy for them, even if I am losing my anger. I do not yet forgive them for anything they have done. If they die, I will not mourn them—

But some of them must know this.

Some must sense it.

Were they not once animals, too?

Have they never let themselves sense the rhythms of the world?

I swim and I sing and my mind seems to expand a little every day, to take up more of my body, even as my stomach shrinks and my blubber melts away.

I feel I am becoming my true self, a being made of my mind, made of my voice, and whenever I let myself wonder how many sunrises I have left, I ache, I grieve, I want to scream out in rage—

But I am more than this fear.

I am part of a great tale, the ending of a legacy. My life will end, but the story itself will not.

I am here. I have been here.

Part of me will always be here.

I swim. I sing. I live. For just a little while longer, I live.

15

When rain comes to the ocean on a calm day, it feels like another world is brushing against ours. It is stunning. One need only turn enough to look up and they will see the old surface transformed; gone are the smooth planes or even the rolling chaos of waves, the undulating swells; in their place, there are tiny explosions, daggers, puffs of air and fingers of silver stabbing down.

This day is a quiet one. I swim near the surface, breathing often. I have gone farther north and the water is colder here, cold enough that I am almost uncomfortable now with my depleting blubber, but I revel in it. This gray day is a day of silence and rain and still water, and my exhalations are the loudest sound.

Out of respect for the rain, wanting to hear its song, its hissing and tinkling against the sea, I cease my cries. I swim and enjoy this unique melody, listening, experiencing. For a while, I enjoy being alone in this place—

But then I realize that I should not be alone here. Not even close. I am somewhere that should be deafening.

I'm alone, but this water is not empty.

This water used to belong to *them*.

There are buoys, chains thick with rust and marine growth. Old debris, old pollution, a few derelict vessels left to anchor where they never would have before. The closer to land I swim, the more there is. It shocks me, but what shocks me most is that all of it is just that: old. Barnacles and seaweed have claimed it.

What happened here? Humans usually clean those things away periodically, and humans are never quiet. There is always an engine, a motor, something beeping, clanging, some sort of waste spilling into the sea.

I swim in closer and I find the entrance to a marina. The marinas I know are deafening places, places of loud music, louder engines, laughter, screeching, things being thrown into the water, poison washed in with every rainfall. The marinas I know are never silent.

There are boats here. So many boats. They wait obediently in their places along the docks. Looking up at them, moving carefully below, I marvel to see so many of them, all abandoned. Their shapes remind me of whale bodies, but that is where the resemblance ends. The weight of barnacles is already beginning to pull some of them down; the sea is claiming them inch by inch. Seaweed bedecks others, seaweed and algae and scum.

What happened to this northern land? Why are the creatures changing here, why are the boats abandoned? I can see that there must have been many humans here once. They must have come to this beautiful, cold, northern port to take their pictures and drink their drinks and shriek and eat, but they are gone now.

I surface in a long avenue between boats, then spyhop.

Nothing. No humans.

The rain is mixed with snow. It makes sloppy pellets that splatter on my face. I am motionless, spellbound.

Sails hang from masts, tattered and frayed by the sun, the rain, and the wind that ate through their furled covers. Rigging has gone to rust. Here and there, masts and radar have broken and no one has fixed them.

Moss grows on some of the boats. Birds have nested. Mussel and clam shells lie shattered along every flat surface; the seagulls have reclaimed this place and there is no one to sweep away the mess.

There are no electric lights.

There are no noisy cars.

There are no engines.

There is silence.

I see a certain word repeated in many places, Seward, but it means nothing to me. Is it a name? A caution? Is that what happened here? It is on the boats, it is on a carved wooden sign, it is everywhere.

The silence chills me, but I stay there looking as long as I can, until it becomes too unnerving. I sink below the surface, unsettled, and let myself drift down to the bottom of the marina. It is just deep enough here for this to feel comforting, despite the detritus of the years that has accumulated there, and I shiver as I think of the silence above.

That is what the silence in the sea will be like when I am gone.

Haunted empty air, haunted empty sea.

I do not understand.

I am not sure I want to.

I watch the rain at the surface and feel a strange dread of it. It is still beautiful, but now it is associated with this empty place, this empty promise—

An emptiness and finality that will claim me. My acceptance falters, fear flutters.

Is this what finality looks like?

Rain unfelt, music unheard, water dancing unseen?

Eventually I flick my tail carefully and move on, exploring all of the marina, looking for life, looking for any sign that I am wrong, that the humans did not abandon this place entirely, but there is nothing. There are the whale-like shapes of boats, there are shadows, there are ghosts locked in by the old shapes of things that once had meaning, and there is the sleet.

When I surface again, I am sure no one will look at me. I float there, feeling the sleet pepper down against my rubbery skin, and I let myself go very, very still. Soon, the water around me is still as well. No waves. No currents. If I do not move, it will be as if I am not here at all.

This is a quiet place.

I shiver. Tiny ripples spread out from me. This wakes me from the strange reverie and I become a whale again, stop myself from becoming one of these ghosts. As I start moving, I see something else moving as well, a flash of something dark above me. I turn my body to see it better, and watch as an eagle alights upon a building.

It looks strong. Beautiful. Dark feathers on its body, broad wings, a gleaming white head. It ruffles its feathers and stretches a wing, then turns its head, clearly watching me. Our eyes lock.

You live? I try to ask it, unsure it if can hear me, uncertain it will want to.

I live, it replies, its bold eyes fixing sharply on me. *What happened here? Why is it so quiet?*

The eagle doesn't answer me for a long moment, and when it does, the message cuts me like coral.

What must happen to all life? An end came. But remember, gentle one, that endings happen all the time. Where one thing ends, another begins. Do not fear. There will be new things here.

And what has been lost? I ask. *What's the price for being without humans?*

What has been lost has been lost. What is gone, is gone. This is the way of living things. This is the way of life itself. Do not fear. Remember, feel, live, but do not fear. Everything dies. Cities, species. Everything but life itself.

I watch as the eagle flies away, and as it does it lets out the sweetest cry, trilling notes so pure they cut into my soul like raindrops against the sea.

I watch until he is out of sight, then I sink below, down under the reach of the sleet, down into the gloomy, quiet, dark waters, and I swim out of the marina.

I do not fear.

I mourn, but I do not fear.

Do I?

When the marina is far behind me, although I know I am still in waters that once belonged to humans, that once teemed with them, I begin singing again.

I start slowly, my mood tempered by the gloominess of the day, but the note of *hope* is as sweet as the eagle's cry, and it encourages me. I try to mimic his cry, to capture that delicate trill.

Soon, I am singing out as loud as ever, letting my voice dance out into the water, letting it spiral into these forgotten places, reverberate off of relics and memories, bringing the sound of the eagle into the soul of the sea, weaving it in with my other songs.

Moonlight. Memory. Mourning.

Hope. Grief. Loss.
Life.
When I sing, am I fighting to live? The thought leaves me with uncertainty, even as it makes me burn with determination to live—

To *live*.

Before I die, I must live.

16

The water gets colder as I go on, but it also becomes cleaner still, which helps me shake off the memory of the haunted marina.

Swimming here feels wonderful, and for a little while I feel like myself again. I feel like a living creature who wants to keep on living, and I feel a pang of hunger, but I am not tempted to eat. I remember the Bay of Life and the fjord; this is not my world anymore. I will not consume the lives of others to continue living in it, even if I can still find joy here.

Lost in thought, I am unaware of my surroundings. Such carelessness was dangerous once upon a time, but there is so little danger in the sea now that I do not remember to be cautious. I swim headlong into something hard bobbing along on the surface.

The impact is not especially painful, but it surprises me. I twist away, staring at this strange white lump.

At first, I do not recognize it. Looking up, I see more small objects floating on the surface, irregular silhouettes against the light. I watch them for a moment, trying to determine what kind of pollution they are, but then I see the tiny shimmers around their edges and something begins to click. It takes me longer than it should to remember what these shapes are, but when I do, I race forward in excitement.

Ice!

The pieces are small, but they are ice! Real ice!

I feel like a foolish calf as I nose along one, rubbing my face on it, enjoying the harshness and the coldness of its bite, enjoying the smoothness, the slickness, enjoying pushing it around. I play with it shamelessly, joy lighting my heart, and as I push the piece of ice around, feeling like a dolphin, everything else falls away. There are no worries, no fears; there is no grief, no heartache. There is just this moment of happy playing, of mindless delight, because *ice* seems like such a rare thing.

When I finally calm down, I remember that the ice must have come from somewhere. This is not sea ice; this is a chunk from a glacier. I look around and soon discover many more pieces of them floating, little bits, larger chunks, and they lead me down another fjord.

This one is not so daunting. It is wider, a more natural shape, and the seawater flows smoothly into it. There is room to swim and the high walls look gentler than the walls of the other fjord; they do not block the sun.

There are more and more pieces of ice. They knock against each other, rattling and thudding and squeaking as the slow swells roll in from the Gulf. I swim under them. The day is overcast, but there is still enough light that even under the ice, it is beautiful. Swimming under the shadows of ice is so very different than swimming in the shadows of the trash caught in the Pacific gyre; the almost-beauty of the trash is only a pale imitation of this place.

The closer I get to the end of the fjord, the more dangerous I sense the water is, but I don't care. There is a tension here, a hint of potential danger, the subtle singing of the earth and the ice as the glacier continues its slow slide into the sea, gracefully moving towards its inevitable demise. It could break off and crush me, bruise me, batter me, but I swim recklessly close.

When a glacier breaks, it calves. The calves become new things of beauty, set free into the ocean.

In this way, we are the same. It seems there are still a few more calves to be born into the sea.

The ice is like a wall. Below the water it is mixed with stone, but above? Above, it is sheer and stunning, and even in the cool gray light of this northern day, there are pockets of vibrant blue. All around me, the water is a stunning blue-green, rich with sediment. It feels like an honor to be here. When I exhale, my breath does not sound loud and out of place; it sounds beautiful, in perfect harmony with the singing of the glacier, the humming of the earth, the softness of gentle swells, the quiet tapping and knocking of small growlers and larger chunks—the glacier's calves—running into each other.

This place makes me feel beautiful.

This place feels like the eagle's song.

I dive deep, for the wild water calls to me.

When I reach the bottom and look up at the faintly gleaming surface, the light seems like the most precious of things, delicate and fragile, the sweetest silver glow in the green and the blue, broken only by the shattered ice.

I yearn for more ice. I yearn for *sea* ice, for icebergs, for unending sheets of ice, for mighty giants born of the coldest place imaginable, but this place is still beautiful.

Slowly, I return to the surface. I breathe, swimming sedately along, feeling ice bump against me. It is chilly, but it is friendly. I do not care if it bruises or scratches me.

When I am far enough away from the wall of ice and stone that it feels safer, I dive again. I only go down deep enough to be surrounded in the dim sweetness of the ocean, and then I hang there, under the edge of light. Ice-shadows fall around me. I let the world move around me in its gentle pace, learning its rhythm.

Once I understand the spirit of this place, once I feel it, I slowly begin to sing.

I sing to the glacier. I sing to the stone. I sing to the ice floating above me, to the minerals in the water.

I sing to this place, to this moment, inviting it to become a part of *my* song, as I have now become a part of its.

Perhaps no one will ever know that I was here, will never know I swam up to the end of this beautiful inlet and saw the ice and understood how rare and lovely it was, but the ocean will know. The ice will know. The stone will know.

Remember me, I sing.

Remember me. Remember my people.

Remember.

My voice echoes strangely here. The fjord is narrow enough for it to echo back at me, to reverberate, and I hear it bouncing off of the ice, off of the walls.

I can feel the song, feel the vibrations dancing along my skin as if it did not come from me at all, but came instead from this tender place, this delicate mix of ice and stone and sea. Perhaps humans once came here and called this beauty raw or brutal, but to me, it is so delicate, so fragile, that it is precious beyond words.

The clouds part. The sun brightens. The ice shadows darken and the water glows brighter and brighter, a vibrant, living, incredible green.

My voice swells with the light.

Yes, I answer to the sunlight's unspoken gift, to these eternal but ephemeral shadows. *Yes. Yes.*

We are here.

When I finish singing, I hear a crack, a rumble. There is a groan, then a growl, and I surface. I know what it must be and I wish to see it happen.

Part of the glacier cracks. Ice sprays into the air like a fine dust, and then there is a mighty crash as a piece of ice as large as I am sloughs off and crashes into the sea. More and more ice follows it, some large but mostly pieces so fine they flow like liquid. They churn up the water, turning it from green to gray, and a wave comes towards me. I remain still, watching.

As the wave surrounds me, visibility below the surface turns to nothing, but I do not mind. Crystals of ice scrape along my skin. Larger pieces roll to the surface, where once the water clears, they too will cast their beautiful shadows and make their beautiful song.

Break by break, this glacier joins the sea. I feel lucky to have witnessed this moment.

I wait for the churning and the surging to be over, then look at the glacier one last time.

Do not hurry into the sea, beauty. Your path is inevitable and perhaps your end is in sight, for no doubt you were once far mightier than you are now, but do not hurry into the sea. You have a voice. You have movement. You are glory and joy.

Do not rush into silence.

17

I swim back towards the open water of the Gulf. On my way, swimming past a few larger pieces of ice, I see a thin form dart through the water, then shoot up onto one of the ice chunks. Knowing what it must be, I surface carefully, not wanting my appearance or displacement to rock the ice too much.

I don't want to frighten her.

I look at the seal and she looks back at me. She is beautiful, her pelt a shining silver, the black spots dark and soft, her eyes softer still, but she is too thin. The thinness makes it heartbreakingly easy to see that she is pregnant.

She watches me with earnest eyes. I want to speak to her, but what could I say? That I wish her well with her baby, that I will not live to see it born, and that perhaps neither will she, but that the world is still a beautiful place? It is beautiful, especially here, beautiful and wild and delicate—

Like her.

Beautiful and wild and delicate.

Perhaps her pup will be one of the newer lives, subtly changed. Perhaps it will thrive. Perhaps it will come into this world knowing the softness and comfort of a mother's love, not knowing that its mother is likely also one of the last of her kind, and perhaps it will remember her. Perhaps it will grow fast and strong, adapting to the new world, a world of less fish, a world where the glacier crawling into the sea is nearly at its end.

Perhaps the pup will thrive.

Perhaps it will not.

Perhaps some of the softness in her eyes is the softness of grief, of acceptance, the softness of a mother who already loves what grows within her yet knows she does not have enough strength left to see it through.

What could I sing to her that would not be disrespectful?

What could I say?

I move closer. She, too, moves closer. She stretches towards the edge of the ice, extending her whiskers forward, her nostrils opening. She sniffs me, touching the side of my face, and I feel honored. I am grateful.

Thank you.

Her touch means more than perhaps either of us could ever say.

I sink below and resume swimming back out to the open. I will not forget her as long as I live.

Hopefully, even after.

I will not forget.

When I reach the open ocean, I begin singing again, and this time it is the mourning song, a mourning song for all the sea, for all I love, with soft little moments of tender hope dashed in, scattered like velvet spots on a sweet, lonely, wide-eyed seal.

18

Another day comes, then another and another.

I am chilled. It is too cold here for a whale as thin as I have become, but it is lovely too, so I do not turn back. I enjoy this, and still feel that I have not gone far enough, that there is somewhere else I need to reach.

Besides, there is something clean feeling in singing into this cold emptiness.

Today, it snows. I have not seen such a heavy snowfall before and it captivates me. The flakes are large and fat and soft and there is very little wind.

I float along, my back out of the water, letting the snow patter down upon me, tender little kisses that vanish all too quickly. It makes the sweetest sound upon the sea's surface, even sweeter than the rain, a delicate little hiss, the pat-pat-pat of tiny hearts.

I focus on the snow as I swim into a large, wide-mouthed bay, and I am so focused that at first I do not hear the buzz.

Buzz.

The buzzing becomes a droning, then a roar, and then all at once I understand what it is:

A motor.

A boat.

Panic shoots through me. A boat is racing towards me, small and lightweight, skimming rapidly across the surface. I dive without thinking, and only when I am down deep enough to feel safe do I look up at the dimly gleaming surface above me.

The boat stops. It is very small, maybe two porpoises long, and it seems to be the kind with a firm shell underneath and soft puffy sides. The sea goes quiet as the engine is shut off. I stare, my heart pounding. Will they kill me? There must be humans in there. Do they want to kill me, to take my blood and my meat, to be disappointed at my lack of blubber, to silence my song in blood and pain?

They float.

I float.

I do not want to swim away in a rush. The tidal current is strong and I am weak, tired; I would have stopped to sleep in this bay, enjoying the snow, enjoying my sense of safety—

False safety.

I watch them.

My lungs hurt.

I did not breathe deeply before I dove.

They do nothing. They wait. Then, when the pressure inside me begins to turn into something else, into a black fire burning through my lungs, I see a tiny little paw, a hand, reach down into the water. The hand has something in it, a metal cup. They shake it and the metal rattles in an oddly pleasing way.

Is this... an invitation?

I have to surface. I *have* to.

It could be a trick, but that odd little clanging noise is not unpleasant. It does not feel hostile.

But the price if I am wrong...

Frightened, ashamed of myself for being frightened when I thought I had left fear behind long ago, I surface slowly, some distance away from them. I exhale loudly, I breathe deeply, and although I could dive again, I do not. Trembling, I nervously wait to see what they will do.

They shout. They talk. One is screaming like a gull, the cries strange—they sound shocked and elated. Happy. *Ecstatic.* There is laughter, there is more talking, and then one of them stands.

I tense, waiting for a harpoon—

But the male undresses. He peels all of his clothing off. The female with him is laughing and crying. She reaches up to steady him. Her hand is beautiful and slim and golden-brown. They both have long hair, long and black and luxurious.

He dives into the water, clumsy as a baby seal navigating its first rough day. The female cries out, gasping, and she looks at me in worry—

She thinks I will hurt him!

They *fear* me.

They fear me, but they are happy to see me? I do not know what to make of this. He is swimming towards me and I am nervous, but something compels me not to move. After a moment, the female undresses and jumps into the water as well.

I let them come to me, these two children of the land, and when they reach me they are both huffing and puffing, their skin pink from the cold. They both sound breathless as they laugh and speak, but their voices are more hushed now, almost reverent. I do not know what they want, but then they both place their hands on me—

And my heart breaks.

I feel it.

We do not share a language, but I feel it.

They love me.

Not only that, but they *understand* me.

They understand that I am the last.

They speak in soft words. They touch my skin. They pat me, they swim alongside me. The woman sings something gentle and soothing, a song any mother would sing to her calf, and my tensions bleeds away. I cannot fear this. I cannot resist this. I ache, I ache so fiercely it seems my heart must come apart; there is nothing sweeter than to be loved when one believes themselves to be lost.

They swim alongside me. They touch me and even climb onto me, their cold little bodies clumsy in the water. I feel tiny, hard-fingered, clawless little hands exploring my fins, then my flukes, and I hold very still, obliging them. I do not understand this. They are humans, and so they are a part of the great evil that befell the world—

But they are kind.

They are loving.

They know that I am the last.

They respect me.

They grieve for me. They grieve with me. Their delicate little bodies must be freezing in this water, freezing on this snowy day, yet here they are, communing with me in the only way they can.

When my shock eases, I find my voice. The first notes are stammering and awkward, but when the humans realize I am singing, they both go silent and still, floating alongside me, holding onto me. They duck underwater often, and then the male floats on his back so he can breathe and listen at once.

They will not understand, I tell myself, trying not to hope, but I sing the song of moonlight, and then the song of morning. I sing the song of hope—and then I sing the song of my own death.

The saltwater upon their faces is not from the sea. I know this when I finish, when they move to look into my eyes. We stare into each other's eyes, into each other's souls, and they weep quietly for me. Tender, tiny arms are laid against my body. They weep, and then they sing something together, something so sweet and kind and loving that although their voices are small, although their voices are limited, I feel their song touch my heart. It becomes a part of my song. A part of me.

I am overwhelmed. I listen. I let myself love them, love these small bodies, these fragile bodies that hold hearts far bigger than I ever knew.

The snow stops falling. The wind increases. The male is shivering hard now, and I realize they are colder than they should be. They must know it too, for they turn to look for their boat, but the tide has taken it from them. The woman looks at the shore, but it is farther away than perhaps they can swim. They worry, I can hear that in their voices as they speak to each other, can hear that they are trying to decide what to do—

I can hear them trying to accept death.

No, sweet ones, you do not end here. You would not regret it, I think. You would consider it worthwhile, an honor to die in the water beside me, just for the chance to touch me, to sing with me, but you will not die today.

They are still holding onto me and so I begin to move, swimming towards their boat. They both let go at once, perhaps frightened, thinking I will dive, and so I go still as well.

The woman speaks. The man listens. Tentatively, they place their shivering hands on my back. They crawl onto me as best they can. They are tense now. Perhaps they fear what I can do to them; despite weakening day by day, despite wasting away, I am far stronger than they could ever be. Perhaps this worries them, but they needn't fear. They love me. I can never harm them.

I swim towards their boat.

The female is the first to realize what is happening. She starts weeping and she presses her face against me. She says something again and again, and although I do not know the words, I know what she is saying.

Thank you.
Thank you.

Their engine catches. They move slowly away from me, back towards the shore. I raise my head out of the water, wanting to see them for as long as I can. They both turn to look at me, shivering, dressed, and as one, they raise their hands.

Perhaps it means love.

Perhaps it means goodbye. Perhaps it is some sort of silent promise.

It means something. This I know.

I turn and dive, and as I do, I raise my flukes into the air, returning their farewell with a slow, graceful one of my own.

This is what I can give. This is my love, my acknowledgment of what we shared.

This is my goodbye.

Remember me.

I wait underwater, knowing that if I surface again they will stop, they will linger too long, and they will be too cold to live. I would like to see them longer, would like to hear their voices, to feel their little hands, to see their tender bodies swimming so clumsily but with such courage and determination through the water to get to me again, but I cannot. I will not risk their lives.

Not for the sake of love.

I listen until I cannot hear the boat anymore, and then I continue on my way.

In some way, some way I do not yet understand, I am changed.

I will never forget their hands upon me, their tears, their voices, all as sweet and free as the kiss of the seal.

19

The moon is setting. I am far enough from land that I cannot hear the waves, although the night is so calm that perhaps there are not many. The moon is golden and beautiful and bright, a mere crescent of light hovering above the edge of the world. The sky is clear. I float on the surface, watching—

And am startled by something fluttering in front of the moon. I was almost asleep, but now I am staring, trying to figure out what it was. It flutters past again, then again, and I realize it is a winged creature. A moth. It is no bigger than one of those feathery snowflakes, and it must be fluttering about me believing I am a place for it to rest, but the moth is doomed. It is too far from land, and something about the unsteadiness of its flight tells me it is weary.

I understand.

I too am weary. I too am doomed.

Watching it saddens me and I start to sink, not wanting to watch those delicate little wings inevitably cease to beat, not wanting to see it fall to the ocean where it will make no more impact than a thought. Or worse, to land; I do not want to see it attempt to land on a sliding panel of moonlight, a shimmering mirror of water. The moth is fluttering low above the smooth water now and seems to be considering just that, and I am almost ready to go, but then it rises again.

It is held in the crescent of the moon, this tiny, delicate life, and I am reminded of the sweet humans. The moth is far more fragile. It is missing one antenna. Its wings look battered and ragged, almost clear. It looks luminous and beautiful and I cannot let it die.

I wait for it to land on me, and as if it senses that I am willing, it quickly does. I cannot feel it well, it weighs far too little, but I sense something moving near my blowhole and I tell myself to believe it is the moth.

Don't go in the water, little one. This ocean is too big for you, and the only one who will remember you will soon be gone.

I swim carefully, trying not to let the water wash over my back, trying not to do anything to dislodge or destroy this tiny life. It is perhaps foolish to attempt to save this creature I can barely feel and can no longer see, especially when my energy is running so low these days, but it cannot be wrong. It can never be wrong to try and save a life, even the soft, tiny, gentle life of a moth.

When I make it to shallow waters I wait, floating. I believe it has left, but I cannot be sure, and that frustrates me. I give a few warning notes, low and powerful ones meant to vibrate my body, and I bob a few times, a little lower in the water each time.

Are you gone? Please be gone. Please be flying off into the night.

There is nothing more I can do to warn it if it is still there.

The moon is only a tiny curved claw above the horizon now. I look at it – and something tiny flutters in front of it.

It could be a single solitary snowflake, a lost leaf, or one beautifully insignificant living creature.

I choose to believe the latter, and to believe that it is not so insignificant after all.

The ocean closes around me, silken smooth as I dive down, seeking a comfortable depth in which to rest. My lullabies surround me, songs I can sing now even in my sleep, softened into a new gentleness by this long day, by the touch of caring hands, by witnessing the delicacy of a life in peril.

The lullabies feel beautiful.

I feel beautiful.

Beautiful and transparent, rocking myself to sleep with songs that will leave the world with me, no matter how desperately I try to give them to the sea.

There is beauty in saving a life, but perhaps there is beauty in impermanence, too.

There is peace in acceptance, and there is a subtle but sublime joy in weaving the world into my songs, in becoming one.

20

For many days and nights, I do not stop singing at all, even when I sleep. Soon enough, though, I stop sleeping. I swim and float and sing, singing out every song, every noise, every name, everything I have ever experienced, everyone I have ever known, singing all of it out into the ocean, my voice growing and growing in beauty and clarity even as I myself am fading away, melting away.

The cold water leaves me shivering, but the air is cleaner here, cleaner all the time. This does not make it clean, the north is not the glorious refuge it once was, but it is better than any other place I might go.

One morning, I sense something different in the water, an excitement, a tension. There are noises up ahead, noises that draw me to them, and I break off my singing to listen to them.

Squeaks.
Clicks.
Cracks.
Growls.
Thuds.
Whines.
Squeals.
Bubbles.
These should be the sounds of life, but they are not.
These are the sounds of ice.
Sea ice.
My heart yearns for it and I swim faster, faster. The sun has not yet risen and my world is dark, but those sounds burst in my mind like radiant light.

I find the edge of the ice field just as the sun rises. Looking at it, my heart soars. Joy pulses through me and I rush to the surface.

The sea and sky go from pale nothingness, the pale silver of promise, and into tender color. Pink and gold and a delicate lavender spread across the world, reflecting and dancing off of the water—

And off of the ice.

For miles and miles, there is ice.

Most of it is small, but some pieces are larger than I am, and some are like mountains to me. They are not what they once were—the top of the world was once a frozen place, a place so cold and clean and wonderful that it was a promise to all of us who dwelled in the sea that life would go on, life eternal—but they are still beautiful. These mighty icebergs, these growlers, the strangely rounded pieces, the patches of frazil that tinkle like tiny bells and flow like oil and yet hold and refract the light in the most enchanting ways, all are stunning.

This is even more beautiful than the Bay of Life, even though I am the only living thing here.

I watch the sun rise. I watch the light spread. I watch the ice gently bobbing. When I dive, I find myself shivering, the cold of the water biting deeply into me, harsher now, but I do not care. This is beautiful. This is why I have made the journey north. This is why I have stayed alive.

I dive deep.

The sound of the ice surrounds me.

I revel in it. I squeak back at the squeals, I click back at the cracking sounds. I dance and sing and make silly noises as a calf would, and although my heart aches with the loneliness, it aches now too for the loveliness it sees, for the place my soul so long thirsted for. I swim through shadows of ice. I weave through pillars under the water. I skim alongside mighty underwater mountains, frozen creations, pockmarked and striated and lonely and blue and white and green and mine. Mine. Mine.

This beautiful place is mine today.

I swim through the ice and do not encounter another living soul, but it is no matter.

This frozen place is my freedom.

This frozen place is my answer.

Life is still worth living, even for the dying.

Beauty is still worth experiencing.

This voyage was worth making.

Excitement builds and builds within me, making me hum with energy I thought my failing body no longer possessed, and when I find a place in the ice that is open enough, I do not stop to think about what I am doing. I charge towards the surface, throwing all of my joy into this movement, all of my hope, all of *me,* and I break through.

I fly into the cold air, the clean air. Water sprays off of me, rainbow droplets freezing as they fall. I hang motionless for a moment, seeing all of this beautiful world, feeling all of this beautiful joy, and then I crash back down into the coldness and the wonder. The force of it hurts my tired body, but I dive deep again. I race up again. I breach again and again and again, diving and leaping and playing and *living* here, in this beautiful end of this beautiful world.

When I am too exhausted to go on, I lay alongside an iceberg. It does not know or care that I am here, that I exist, but this does not matter. I lay alongside it and listen to the ice creaking and moving and groaning within it, all the tiny sounds of change and time, and although the ice does not know that it is melting, I know that it will never be more beautiful than it is in this moment.

I am exhausted. I'm shivering. I look out at the clear water all around me. Everything here is blue, blue in all directions, blue, blue, blue, the richest blue water, the darkest blue shadows of ice, the blue undersides, the brilliant blue cracks, and the blue promise of the sky above.

I shiver and shiver. My body aches from the exertion. I feel my death waiting for me in my joy, but I will not give in yet. I could. I could die here, I know. I could simply give up, could let myself sink, but I will not. Not yet. This place is my promise, my haven, my answer; this place, this ice, is my peace.

My anger is gone now. My resentment is gone. My grief is gone. I no longer mourn. I feel nothing but weariness and joy, joy as deep and as endless as all the ocean. The ice fields will melt. The Arctic will perish.

These things cannot be stopped—but while they are here, they can be celebrated, and I celebrate them.

I shiver and sing and listen and live. I am more acutely aware of my own heart than I have ever been, feeling its every beat, feeling its strength pumping blood through me.

The ice sings with me. It echoes my cries and chirps its own. It shifts and moves and trembles as if it possesses its own life, its own story.

When I have recovered, I swim through it again, gently this time, careful, and I take in every last drop of beauty my soul can possibly hold.

At sunset, I am out of the ice.

I return the way I came.

I spyhop. I watch the sun lowering, transforming into its rich pinks and reds. I watch the gleaming, shifting ice field, the shimmering of the air, the sparkling of the water. I watch it all, my heart pained with the beauty, overwhelmed with it, and I wish I could live forever, live forever in this moment, live forever in this beautiful place—

But the sun must set and the ice must melt and my story, too, must have its ending.

The sun seems to flame and flare before it sinks, and in those final moments, all the life and joy of my heart coalesces into a flame just as bright, just as pure. Then I too sink into the water.

I turn south, leaving behind the sweet singing of the ice, and I begin my long voyage home.

21

Everything is different now. Somehow, the world seems both smaller and sweeter. I am always cold, always weary, but I find new strength, enough to go on, enough to keep swimming, enough to know I will make it.

I do not sing now, saving my voice, my energy, I simply swim, but the song continues within me. I can feel the melodies and the magic as a part of my blood, my body. I am my song, now that I have found this peace, the strange and inexplicable gift of the ice.

The journey south seems to take much longer than the journey north, but I pay little attention now to the day and the night. I do not eat, nor do I sleep; I am caught somewhere in between waking and dreaming, content to be here, my mind drifting as I swim, as I take in every sound for the last time, every current of cold water, every raindrop sparkling the surface, every icy wind that ruffles it.

At times, it feels as if my body is transparent, no different from a jellyfish, but I know that is not true. My body is still solid, still alive, and although it weakens and grows thin, although I shiver, it is still here, still housing my mind, my soul.

I swim.

I listen.

I take in the world around me, trying to find beauty in every minuscule thing, even the things I did not notice before. I look for the riots of color, for the rippling and blurring as fresh and salt water meet, for the shimmering edges of temperatures layered atop each other. I take note of every other living creature, and although I do not sing to them or greet them, I remember them. Each one becomes a part of me, and with every life I see, even as I myself diminish, I feel as if I am expanding, spreading out somehow, becoming a part of them as well.

Dying is a sad and lonely thing, but now, before the grief, there is a newer appreciation for beauty, a depth of love for it I had never felt before. It is not humble to believe I have found wisdom in my journey, but it is also not shameful.

One is allowed to believe in transcendence.

22

Night has already fallen by the time I reach the Bay of Life. I am surprised to be here, for I cannot tell how long it has been; perhaps the blurring of time is an effect of my failing body; the mind, the spirit, and the flesh are all beginning to move at different speeds.

The night is rough, or at least rough to me; waves that I might once have played in now jostle me at the surface. I am helpless to resist them, so I do not go near the rocks that make up the bay's entrance.

For a moment I regret this choice, because I would like to go in there, but I suspect that if I enter the bay, I will never leave it again. I do not wish to pollute that place by dying in it; yes, the creatures there would scavenge my flesh and take life from it, but it somehow feels wrong. That bay is too important to me, too beautiful; I do not want to sully it with my death.

Shivering and weak, I lay deep and listen to the waves as they pound against the rocks, listen to the water rushing and flooding through that narrow opening and into that beautiful cradle of change. I listen, and when I have heard enough, I decide that it is my time to sing again.

I am not sure how long it has been since I left the true north, since I left the ice on that glorious day, but the sound of my voice startles me. It is so much bigger than I ever knew, rich and full and sweet and poignant, and I take comfort in all of its beauty.

Is it so strange to find part of myself truly beautiful, even as I waste away?

It cannot be wrong to enjoy such a thing.

I sing to the bay, letting my voice and my hopes and my dreams all flow into that water. In this way, I try to bless this place, to bless this life. I give them all that I am, all I have seen, all I have loved, and this giving is a prayer: care for this place well, Ocean, nurture this tiny spark of life.

When my voice has echoed for the last time off of the rocks, when the waves grow too rough above me, I say goodbye to the beautiful little bay.

I will never see it again.

23

The warm southern water is a comfort when I reach it. Everything that I remembered is still there, the trash, the dangers, the listlessness of the water, the ugliness of the shore, the glow against the sky, but the water itself is warm. It eases my shivering and my pain and although the water here does not have the same living joy as the chilled currents of the north, it is home.

I was born here, and now my story will end here.

I will be complete.

The Arctic was beautiful. The day of ice and sunlight gave me more joy than I have felt in a long time. I would have been happy if I stayed there, but it would not have been right.

Besides, I did not want the humans who loved me in the north to find my body one day and be crushed.

Perhaps that is a kinder desire than the human race deserves, but they were sweet and kind and beautiful in their way, and my heart has changed since the night I raged against all of this loss.

No, I could not have remained in the Arctic to die. I believe that the changes happening to creatures in the north will give them a chance to live in a new world—

I want my death to happen in the old one.

Perhaps no one will ever know it, but this will be my last act of defiance. Let my body remind any humans who come across it of just what they have done, let them see the cost of all their crimes.

Let my body feed the creatures who cannot make epic journeys across oceans.

Let the end of my story, the end of my people, mean something.

I have had beauty, drunk deeply of its comforts, plunged into its joy. I have known the sweetest of all light; I can end in darkness.

There is nothing to fear now. Nothing at all.

A shark swims with me.

A sea lion darts alongside me.

A school of fish surround me in the sunlight and swim at my slow and weary pace for as long as they can.

From everywhere I encounter, I feel it.

Respect.

Grief.

Understanding.

Pride.

They know. They sense my death the same as I, and they know what it means. They know I am the last. They know the ocean is losing something it will never regain.

I take comfort in their love, in the respect they offer; they give me strength, courage.

Golden moonlight seems to hold the shark in a halo as he accompanies me. I am silent, staring at him, taking in his beauty; he is like a ghost, a beautiful ghost drifting along. His skin shows damage—there are hooks caught on him, and a twist of some sort of line is wrapped around one of his pectorals—but he is still beautiful. Radiant above, capturing moonlight filtered through the murky water, dark and shadowy below. His eyes are calm and despite his injury, despite the indignity of the plastic that will slowly kill him, he has his own dark nobility.

It is an honor to swim beside him. The company of this predator gives me one more measure of peace, promises me that it is alright to let go of everything. His smooth movements are gentle, reassuring.

The sea will not forget me, even when I die. It loves me and it grieves for me, with me, but it will not forget, for I will never truly cease to be. The world's last whale will perish, but my spirit will dissipate into something greater.

I will become the sea.

I die, but death is not so silent and painful an ending as I once thought.

24

Pollution had already started, but the water wasn't as bad as this when I was born. Now, at the height of the sea's crisis, the choking mass of garbage feels oddly familiar, homelike in the saddest way.

Plastic drifts against me, listless and lifeless and ugly, the fallout of the war the humans waged against my world without ever needing to declare their intentions. The feeling of it would have made me shiver once, but no longer. Now, I remember the gyre, the place where the garbage was so thick that it darkened the sea. I remember the rotting human bodies floating there and I compare them to the living human bodies that took such joy in seeing me.

The living are far more beautiful than the dead. This is, I think, the case for all life: it is better when it is *alive,* better when it is free.

I am finally able to let myself mourn for those discarded bodies floating with the trash in the ocean.

They had lives once. They were perhaps foolish and selfish, perhaps the type to throw plastic bags and bottles and toys out into the water or onto the beach, or to toss them carelessly into open trash bins where the wind could pluck the garbage out again and scatter it. Perhaps they simply bought everything they wanted, never worrying about what would happen when it became trash in the end, never thinking of the ways they encouraged their massive corporations to produce more and more. Perhaps they bathed in chemicals and scrubbed their clothing with even more, never considering where that pollution went, what would happen when their swollen, engorged cities all did the same things, spitting out the same poisons—

But they lived, once.

They lived and they died.

This, I understand.

This, I have empathy for.

Every life has meaning. Even theirs.

Humans, I railed against you once, furious and betrayed, but no longer. I accept that it is over. I accept that my people are gone. I accept what you have done to the sea.

I accept it. I accept what you are and what I will soon be.

Can you?

Can you remember your own countless dead? Your own mistakes?

Can you face the cost of your thoughtlessness?

Can you remember me?

My mother nursed me here. Her heart was the sound of the world. Her songs were beauty itself. I swam for the first time here, I took my first breaths here.

There is no moon tonight.
The water is still.
I raise my head above it.
All around me, the ocean is made of black glass. If there was moonlight it would turn this glass to gold.

A north wind clears the smog away and I gaze into the stars, into their endless depths, endless colors. They shine down upon the mirror darkness of the sea, upon the human lands, and they shine down upon me. This feels like another blessing, another goodbye, and I take a moment to appreciate it, even if it was unexpected.

The stars are beautiful, but they are not my world. They are not my heart. My eternity awaits me far below, not there in those twinkling lights.

I am nervous. Not afraid, not really, but I feel apprehensive, feel the tension of knowing something new is about to happen. My body is so weak, so frail, that it is a miracle I am here at all, but now as I face the final moments, the final decision, I feel it. I feel the life and beauty of my body, feel its frailty, and I remember its grace from days gone by. I am very fond of all of myself, every inch of skin, every memory, and every scar. I was a beautiful creature once—

I am allowed to love myself for that.

Still, I shiver. Not from the cold, for these waters are so warm that I do not feel it, but from the great unknown, the eternity that will claim me tonight.

I breathe and shiver and wait, struggling with myself, trying to find the courage to go, to take this last dive, to plummet into the depths for the final time. Thoughts intrude, little remnants of the instinct to survive. I consider finding food, finding rest, consider ways to give myself more time, more days—

But what purpose would that serve?

I would suffer. I would be cold. My body aches, and it would ache more. I would suffer in pain and cold and loneliness, having already seen the most beautiful thing there is to see, having already made the one last journey I needed to make.

I struggle and I shiver and then suddenly I am both more frightened and lonely than I have ever been. I let out one keening cry, a cry of misery, of the aching loneliness within.

I wish my mother were here. I wish she could sink with me into the depths, guiding me with her song, with the great warmth of her body. She would soothe my fears and I would be small again and she would tell me that everything would be alright, and I would believe her. To be touched by her one last time, to hear her voice again, to feel her heartbeat in the water between us, this would take the fear away—

But she is not here.

I am alone.

I am alone.

I am alone.

25

I surface one last time. I exhale one last time.
I take my last breath.
I dive.

26

These are my final moments. This is what I have been saving my voice for. Desperately afraid, desperately tired, desperately lonely, I sing—

And my voice is the most beautiful sound in all the world. As if my body has finished melted away from it, removing any barrier, it is resonant and rich and beautiful. It changes the darkness of the water into light, imbuing it with every color.

I do not sing any particular song, for I have already sung them all. I have sung all that I am out into the ocean and given it all away.

Now, trembling, frightened, but understanding, I simply sing as I swim down into the depths. I sing to fill my world with beauty one final time.

I sing to live, even as I die.

Memories flicker like light across my mind, a kaleidoscope of color and sound.

The sky above is dark. I feel a swift and strange sense of elation at having left it behind. The sea around me is darker still, but this darkness cannot hurt me.

Nothing can now.

My fear begins to melt away.

Memories dance in my song, but they are not complete. They are more like dreams, flickering pieces of things I have felt and seen, sparkling seconds of who I have been.

Memories dance. My weak body moves smoothly as I swim down, down, down into the deep, down into a darkness so complete that even a moonless night can never compare.

Memories dance and my voice is a rainbow of light, and when I lose the strength to continue moving, continue swimming, when my exhausted, starved body finally can take me no farther, I go quiet.

I am still alive.

The sound fades.

The lights fade.

Around me, the ocean is black again. Black and rich and deep and endless, the blackest black—

A comforting black.

This is what it looks like at every beginning.

This is what it looks like at every end.

I am grateful to be no different.

I drift. My body is motionless, unable to move again, too weak, but I feel myself floating, slowly sinking, and I sing again.

This time, it is just that one note, the sweetest one I ever learned.

Hope.

I repeat this note again and again, the gift of the last whale, the only thing I have left to offer.

My heart stops beating.

I feel it.

It frightens me. For one moment, I am nothing but fear as I feel this new darkness and stillness inside myself, as my note of hope tapers off—

But the note continues around me.

My body sinks, but I seem to be rising away from it, and the note is growing louder all the time, this single sweet sound, the promise of hope. My body falls away and I look at it, the emaciated and scarred form of the last whale, but then I am looking around me in awe as I feel myself rising, propelled ever upwards.

All around me, the sea is filled with light, that note of hope brightening it, bringing it to life. The light grows and grows until it should be blinding, and then it begins to take shape—

And I see them.

The whales.

My family.

All of them.

All of us.

Light comes from me as well and I sing in a new voice, a voice without sound, a voice perhaps made of the very thing I sing of, a voice of hope. Overjoyed, I swim into this endless light, into the company of my mother, my father, into the company of all those I have ever known, all I have loved—

All I have lost.

I sing, and every other voice sings with me.

Once, I dove in sparkling water, clear and cold, salt but sweet.

I danced in beams of sunlight and my songs raced before me into the unknowable depths of the sea.

The water danced as well, silk against my skin, effervescent, full of life.

I danced in bars of sunlight and seawater, in what will always be sacred, plunging down into the depths, gold and blue and green, an incandescence of life and joy, limitless illumination, light one still had faith in even when it was lost to the depths—

And now, although I am gone, although the ocean will be forever silent, I have escaped. I am free of pain. I am free of the grief of watching the world around me die.

I am free.

You broke my heart, stole my home, and slowly slaughtered my people, but for all of that, you could not shatter my soul.

I pray you may yet save your own.

If you enjoyed this book, if it moved you, it would mean the world to me if you would help get the story out there by leaving a review on Amazon; the more positive reviews, the more Amazon will help other readers find it.

Do you believe that climate change, pollution, and how we deal with trash are an individual or industrial responsibility? Who should be responsible for safeguarding the future of this world, for protecting wild species? What do you see as the most effective ways to make that happen?

If you have any ideas for how people and businesses can help to reduce the impacts of climate change, or even just words of encouragement for those who are trying their best but feeling discouraged, please share them in your review!

Yours, Lisse

Made in the USA
Coppell, TX
09 October 2021